ORCA
YOUNG
READERS

Trouble in the Trees

YOLANDA RIDGE

ORCA BOOK PUBLISHERS

Library and Archives Canada Cataloguing in Publication

Ridge, Yolanda, 1973-
Trouble in the trees / Yolanda Ridge.
(Orca young readers)

Issued also in electronic format.
ISBN 978-1-55469-385-6

I. Title. II. Series: Orca young readers
PS8635.I374T76 2011   JC813'.6   C2010-907918-3

First published in the United States, 2011
Library of Congress Control Number: 2010941959

Summary: When tree climbing is banned at her townhouse complex,
Bree assumes a new role in her community: activist and advocate.

Mixed Sources
Product group from well-managed forests,
controlled sources and recycled wood or fiber
www.fsc.org   Cert no. SW-COC-000952
© 1996 Forest Stewardship Council

*Orca Book Publishers is dedicated to preserving the environment and has printed this book
on paper certified by the Forest Stewardship Council.*

Orca Book Publishers gratefully acknowledges the support for its publishing programs
provided by the following agencies: the Government of Canada through the
Canada Book Fund and the Canada Council for the Arts, and the Province of
British Columbia through the BC Arts Council and the Book Publishing Tax Credit.

Typesetting by Jasmine Devonshire
Cover artwork by Pete Ferguson

ORCA BOOK PUBLISHERS
PO Box 5626, Stn. B
Victoria, BC Canada
V8R 6S4

ORCA BOOK PUBLISHERS
PO Box 468
Custer, WA USA
98240-0468

www.orcabook.com
Printed and bound in Canada.

14 13 12 11 • 4 3 2 1

In memory of my dad,
who always encouraged me to climb to the top.

Chapter 1

I stood on the branch and reached up. It was too dangerous to go up on my tiptoes, so I arched my back and stretched my arms as far as they could go. Up. Up. Up. Just a little higher...

"Brianna Bridges!" Mom's voice shot up from below. "Get down right now."

I lost my balance.

Tumbling forward, I barely managed to grab the trunk of the tree with my outstretched arms. My legs automatically swung forward and wrapped around a branch I couldn't see but knew was there. I looked down and tried to catch my breath.

"Mom! Don't freak out! I'm fine," I called back. Under my breath I added, "At least I was until you showed up."

"Now, Brianna." I could just see Mom through the leaves. She was standing with her feet apart and her arms crossed. She didn't have anything with her except a folded piece of paper, which stuck out from underneath her armpit. A branch blocked my view of her face, but I knew by the tone of her voice that she was wearing her *I mean business* expression—the one that makes her eyebrows scrunch together so tight that the space between them disappears.

"But, Mom, I'm almost at the top," I said, even though I knew this was an argument I wasn't going to win.

"I know. Come down. Now."

"Oh, Mom…" I sighed loudly.

As slowly as possible, I worked my way out of the tree I referred to as Mount Everest. Why did she have to show up just as I was making progress?

"We need to talk," Mom said when my feet finally hit the ground.

"Do we have to talk now? I was almost at the top."

"You're going to have to take a break from tree climbing." She uncrossed her arms and waved the piece of paper in front of my face. "A long break."

"But I need to get to the top of every tree in Cedar Grove."

"You may want to, but you don't need to."

"No, I need to. Tyler doesn't think I can do it, and I know I can." I rolled my eyes. I shouldn't have to explain this to her. Again. Mom knew all about the rivalry between me and Tyler.

"I don't understand why you're so worried about Tyler. You already know that you're the stronger climber." Mom shook her head as she spoke.

"But I need to make sure that he knows it too." I glanced over toward Tyler's bedroom window, which faced the Cedar Grove courtyard and the trees. I didn't want Tyler to overhear me talking about him. And I really didn't want him to know that I gave our rivalry a second thought. That would be bad.

"We're going in. It's time for lunch anyway," Mom replied. She was already walking away.

"Was that the talk we *needed* to have?" I followed her, knowing I had no choice.

"No," she said. "Your dad needs to be in on that one."

As we walked through the front door of our townhouse, Mom said, "You'll never guess where I found her, Steven."

Dad smiled at me from the kitchen. "Up a tree?"

I smiled back at him and nodded.

"If it's got branches, Bree's going to climb it," Dad said as he put a plate of grilled cheese sandwiches on the table.

Mom frowned, but the rest of her face softened as she stood next to Dad, putting one hand on his back and showing him the piece of paper with the other.

"Right," Dad said. The laugh lines on his face disappeared.

"What's this all about?" I said as I sat down at the table. The smell of fried bread and melted cheese made me realize I was starving. I'd been climbing all morning.

"It's about this notice," Mom said.

"I kinda figured," I said. "Has the school finally written to tell you that a child as brilliant as me doesn't need to attend classes regularly? Or did CTV see me climbing and write to ask permission to feature me in an upcoming segment of *Percy's Prospects*?" I smothered my sandwich with ketchup and took a big bite.

Dad, who normally laughed at my attempts at humor, kept his mouth straight. "You're not going to like this, Bree."

"So, what is it?" I asked, swallowing hard. "You guys are acting even weirder than usual."

"It's a notice from the council," Dad answered.

I rolled my eyes. Boring. The Cedar Grove Neighborhood Council was always sending us something. New rules, regulations, reminders…all aimed at making it easier for a large number of people to live so close together. Or so they said. Personally, I was tired of all the bylaws made up by old people who didn't remember what it was like to be a kid.

Last year, the council made it illegal for anyone under sixteen to be in the weight room without adult supervision. That hadn't bothered me too much, but it sure bugged Tyler, who was always trying to hang out with the teenagers. Then they expanded the bylaw to include other common areas, making a bunch of us mad because we could no longer play hide and seek in the storage room or race our skateboards on the smooth, wide asphalt of the parking garage.

I didn't think there was anything left for them to ban. The notice was of no interest to me. I took another big bite of sandwich.

"There's a new bylaw, Brianna," Mom said.

"Surprise, surprise," I mumbled, not looking up from my lunch.

"It's a bylaw against tree climbing."

Now she had my attention.

Chapter 2

I took a sip of milk so I wouldn't choke on my sandwich. "What do you mean, a bylaw against tree climbing?"

"Looks like the other residents of Cedar Grove are as worried about your tree climbing as I am." Mom was still frowning.

Jumping up from my chair, I grabbed the piece of paper off the table. It looked exactly like all the other notices the council sent out.

Dear Residents of Cedar Grove,
This notice is to inform you of a new interim bylaw recently approved by the Cedar Grove Neighborhood Council.

Bylaw 47.21: Tree climbing, defined as any activity consisting of ascending and moving around in one or more trees, is prohibited on Cedar Grove property unless performed by a certified arborist.

All trees within the property line of the Cedar Grove Townhouse Complex are governed by this bylaw.

Please note that this new bylaw is effective immediately. As per Neighborhood Council procedure, this interim bylaw will be ratified at the upcoming Annual General Meeting. In the meantime, any resident found in violation of the bylaw will be fined in accordance with the Neighborhood Act.

Thank you for your attention to this matter.
Sincerely,
Cedar Grove Neighborhood Council

I was stunned. I read the notice twice. No more tree climbing? I was pretty sure that's what they were trying to say. This must be a joke.

"I'm still not sure the council can do that," Dad said.

"Well, I'm sure they can. It's only a matter of time before someone gets hurt climbing those trees," Mom said.

"But that's what kids do. They climb trees," Dad replied. "What's next—a ban on hide-and-go-seek? Or tag?"

"It's dangerous, Steven! I keep saying that! Why aren't you listening to me?" Mom took a step away from Dad and crossed her arms, signaling that the case was closed. Mom and Dad didn't like to disagree, and they worked hard at what they called "united parenting." A little too hard, in my opinion.

I chewed slowly through the rest of my lunch, even though my appetite was gone. How could I stop climbing trees? My mind started racing, trying to think of other places where I could climb. Problem was, we lived right in the middle of Vancouver, one of the most populated cities in Canada, where lots of people were crammed into a small area surrounded by the ocean and the mountains. There weren't a lot of climbable trees around. The ones in the park by the school were all skinny and small. The ones lining the Fraser River pathway had all been trimmed so the lowest branches were too high to reach. And the trees in the field between Cedar Grove and the neighboring townhouse complex? Well, now there weren't any trees there at all. They had been chopped down to make room for the adults to play Ultimate Frisbee.

While I was eating and thinking, I heard the sounds of a street hockey game starting up. Nets were dragged into the street. Hockey sticks scraped against the cement. I went to the window and saw that Tyler and his sidekick, Michael, had already separated everyone into teams. Five players for the Blues. Four players for the Reds.

Over the noise of the hockey game I could hear some girls skipping and chanting: *"Ice-cream sundae, banana split. Salina's got a boyfriend, who is it? A! B! C!..."*

There were five girls, all younger than me, that I privately referred to as the Cedar Grove Girly-Girls. They were always—I mean ALWAYS—skipping. I often went to bed at night with the sound of their rhymes ringing in my head. And all their favorite rhymes were about boyfriends. I had no idea why. I had no interest in boys whatsoever. Not in that way.

I didn't have any interest in skipping either. After about five minutes, I found it boring. All you had to do was jump. Over and over and over again. There was no thinking involved. I guess that's why they spent so much time coming up with those rhymes. And since I wasn't very good at rhyming, I didn't spend much time with the Cedar Grove Girly-Girls.

On the other hand, I loved playing sports with the boys who lived in Cedar Grove. There were always enough people around to start up a game of something. It was the best part about living in a complex like Cedar Grove. The worst part was that everyone always seemed to know all your business.

Leaving the rest of my lunch untouched, I ran to get my shoes so I could join the Reds. They didn't really need another player. Michael was so good at hockey I was sure he could beat all five Blues on his own. But I was anxious for the distraction.

"Hey, Bree," Ethan, Cedar Grove's kid genius, called my name as soon as I stepped outside.

It took me a second to spot him sitting on the steps in front of his house, watching the action. "Hey, Ethan. Why aren't you playing?" I asked.

He shrugged.

Before I could ask him any more questions, one of the other boys yelled, "Bree! Wanna play?"

"You bet," I said grabbing a stick from one of the open garages. "I'll be Red."

"Not afraid to lose?" Tyler was playing goalie for the Blues. As he looked up at me the ball sailed past him into the net.

"Goal!" Ethan yelled. This cheered me up a little. Okay, a lot.

"Time out," Tyler said, glaring at Ethan.

The boys reluctantly followed Tyler's lead, as usual, and the game stopped. Some players took a water break. Others slowly got ready for the next face-off. They didn't stop because they wanted to. They stopped because they thought they had to. At twelve years old, Tyler was the oldest and biggest kid living in Cedar Grove. Not including the teenagers, who never wanted anything to do with us.

"Hope you're not planning on climbing trees anytime soon, Bree." Tyler laughed. "If you do, I'm going to have to report you to the Neighborhood Council."

"What's he talking about, Bree?" Ethan asked.

"Tree climbing is illegal in Cedar Grove now. Your parents could get fined." Tyler sounded pleased, probably because the one activity I could actually beat him at had just been banned.

"The council has banned tree climbing," I mumbled to Ethan, trying not to let Tyler get to me. A fight with Tyler would only make things worse. If that was even possible.

"Really?" Ethan said, his eye's growing wide. "I can't believe it."

"Believe it," Tyler said. "It's true."

A lot of the Cedar Grove kids hadn't heard the news yet. The notice had only just arrived in the mail. Everyone seemed pretty upset. Except Tyler. For sure he was glad I wouldn't be able to get to the top of every tree before him. Before anyone.

"What's the fine?" Michael asked. Michael was eleven—the same age as me—and he acted like the world revolved around Tyler.

"Don't know," I replied. I hadn't thought about that. It didn't really seem to matter. For me, the fact that it wasn't allowed was enough. I wasn't the type to break the rules. Not because I was a goody-goody, but because I was almost certain to get caught.

"Oh, it's probably only a hundred bucks or something," said Tyler. As if he had any idea. "Not enough to stop someone who truly wanted to climb a tree." He smirked at me.

"It's two hundred and fifty dollars for the first violation and five hundred and twenty-five for the second. If you don't pay the fine, the Neighborhood Council can sell your townhouse and keep the money," Ethan said. I was surprised to hear him speak up like that, especially around Tyler. He's usually pretty quiet.

Michael whistled. "That's a lot of money!"

"The fine is nothing compared to being kicked out of your house," said Ethan.

"This sucks," said Peter, one of the boys who liked to climb with me.

"Really sucks," added another.

"Isn't your mom the president of the Cedar Grove Neighborhood Council?" Tyler asked Ethan.

"Uh…yeah," Ethan replied, looking down at his shoes.

"She's sure made things miserable around here. Since she became president we've lost the jungle gym, then the weight room, and now this. What's her problem anyway?"

"Leave Ethan alone," I said. "It's not his fault."

Tyler turned toward me. "You're right. It's your fault, Bree. Always needing to climb higher and higher. Encouraging other kids to take risks. What'd you think the council was going to do?"

I stood there in silence, searching my brain for a quick and clever comeback. Nothing. I looked around at all the other kids. They were all staring at me, waiting for a response.

Was it really my fault? I wasn't sure. But I knew one thing for certain. I was going to have to do something about this tree-climbing bylaw.

Chapter 3

I had to wait until lunch at school the next day to discuss the tree-climbing situation with my best friend Sarah. During the week she lives with her dad and stepmom in a townhouse complex near Cedar Grove, but she spends weekends at her mom's house in Surrey. Even though Surrey's only an hour from Vancouver it feels a lot further because Sarah's mom is really strict about Sarah's phone and computer use.

As we were eating some disgusting thing the cafeteria cooks had tried to disguise as food, I told her all about the letter from the Neighborhood Council and how Tyler had told everyone that the new bylaw was my fault.

Sarah ran her tongue over her braces and then said, "It's not your fault that you're good at climbing trees." That's why Sarah is my best friend. She sees things the same way I do. And when I'm not sure about something, she makes it all seem clear.

"Do you think there's anything I can do about it?" I asked her.

"I don't know, Bree. It's gonna be tough," Sarah said thoughtfully.

"But I have to try, right?"

"Of course." Sarah stuffed a spoonful of slop into her mouth before continuing. "Remember when my dad went to battle with our council over clotheslines?"

I nodded. How could I forget? It had been a big deal in Meadow Park, Sarah's townhouse complex, for a long time.

"He made a presentation."

"Presentation?"

"Yup. In front of the entire council. A PowerPoint presentation. He practiced on me ahead of time. I forget most of it because it, was so long and boring—all 'environmental statistics' and 'technical details.'"

Sarah's dad and stepmom were always trying to reduce their carbon footprint. A while ago, they got on a kick about hanging their clothes outside to avoid using the dryer. Problem was, there was a bylaw against clotheslines in their townhouse complex. And there still is a bylaw against clotheslines in Meadow Park because people who live close together don't want to see each other's underwear flapping around in the wind. Or something like that. Obviously, the presentation hadn't done much good.

"I don't know if I could do a presentation," I said. "Not in front of the entire council. That's like, what? Six or seven grown-ups?" The thought of it made me feel sick to my stomach. I pushed away the rest of my so-called lunch.

"So what are you gonna do then?" Sarah asked, digging into her chocolate pudding.

"Maybe I could just talk to the president of the council?" I said, thinking about Ethan's mom, Ms. Matheson.

"Worth a try," Sarah said as the bell rang. "Let me know how it goes." She gathered her stuff and darted away to class.

I headed off to homeroom, happy to have a plan. I knew I had to do something about the bylaw, but I was a bit nervous. Talking to Ms. Matheson would certainly be easier than giving a presentation to the entire council. She was a mom, after all, and she worked hard to give Ethan a good life. Extra hard because there was no Mr. Matheson. Still, I was just a regular eleven-year-old and Ms. Matheson was a president. Even if she was only president of the Neighborhood Council, she was still a *president*.

I decided not to put it off. As soon as my homework was finished, I summoned up all my courage and knocked hesitantly on the Mathesons' front door, Unit 49.

When Ethan answered, he was holding something against his elbow. It took me a moment to realize that it was one of those Magic Bags. According to the ads, they have some kind of grain inside that can be cooled in the freezer or warmed in the microwave. Relieves pain, helps you relax, takes away stress…blah, blah, blah. As soon as Ethan saw me, he tried to hide the bag behind his back. I made a mental note to ask him about it after I finished talking to his mom.

"Oh, hi, Ethan. Could I, uh, speak to your mom?" I stammered.

"Sure, Bree," Ethan replied. "Do you wanna go out and play catch after?"

"Maybe," I said, trying to look past Ethan into the house. I'd been here lots of times. I'd probably been inside every townhouse in Cedar Grove. The ones with kids anyway. But I'd never felt nervous about it. Until now.

Ethan gave me a funny look and then yelled up the stairs, "Mom!"

"Don't yell at me, Ethan!" Ms. Matheson yelled back.

"Bree's here and she wants to talk to you!" Ethan yelled again, louder this time.

"Who?"

"BREE!"

"Okay. I'll be right down."

Ms. Matheson clomped down the stairs, wearing her work clothes—a suit and uncomfortable-looking high-heeled shoes. Poor Ethan. Not only was his mom the president of the council, she was also the principal of the local high school.

"Hi, Brianna," Ms. Matheson said. She didn't look very welcoming, but she didn't look like she would bite either. "What can I do for you?"

I cleared my throat. "Um, Ms. Matheson, it's about the, um, ban on tree climbing?"

"Yes?" As she lowered her chin and narrowed her eyes, Ms. Matheson suddenly reminded me of our school principal, Mr. Lee. How she managed it, I don't know. There could not be two people on earth that looked less alike than Ms. Matheson and Mr. Lee.

"I'd really like to talk to you about the, um, the tree-climbing bylaw," I mumbled.

"Okay, Brianna," Ms. Matheson replied with a sigh, "but I don't have time right now. Why don't you come and speak to the council? Our next meeting is on Tuesday night at seven thirty. I'll set aside ten minutes to address your concerns." And with that, Ms. Matheson turned and clomped back up the stairs.

I stood there in silence. An image of me standing in front of a huge crowd of grown-ups, giving a PowerPoint presentation full of statistics and technical details, flashed through my head. What had I gotten myself into?

Ethan's voice brought me back to earth. "Can we play ball now, Bree?"

"What?" I looked at Ethan, who was still standing by the door. At some point, he must have dropped the Magic Bag. Now he was holding his ball glove and looking at me expectantly.

"Ball. Do you want to play ball?" Ethan said loudly.

"No baseball, Ethan!" Ms. Matheson yelled down the stairs again. "Your elbow hasn't healed yet!"

"Elbow?" I looked at Ethan, my eyebrows raised.

"It's no big deal, Bree," Ethan said quickly. "Guess I gotta go."

And before I could say another word, he shut the door in my face.

Chapter 4

The next week was torture. The prospect of making a presentation to the Cedar Grove Neighborhood Council turned me into a nervous wreck. And I couldn't climb trees, which is what I normally do to relax.

It wasn't just the size of the council that made me nervous. Or the fact that it was made up of grown-ups who didn't seem to like kids. Or even the fact that my favorite pastime was at stake. Truthfully, the thought of giving any presentation filled me with dread, no matter who was watching or what was at stake.

Part of what made me nervous was the accent I'd picked up from Mom, who immigrated to Canada a year before I was born. She'd met Dad while he was in England playing hockey with the Sheffield Steelers.

Mom had always dreamed of leaving England, so she asked her engineering firm for a transfer to their Canadian office. By the end of that hockey season, Mom and Dad were married and living in Cedar Grove. Now my dad was a hockey scout for the NHL.

Mom's accent was so strong when I was baby that I ended up sounding British too. My accent, like Mom's, had slowly disappeared, but there were still times when I pronounced things like a proper English schoolgirl. I got teased about it a lot, and when it came to presentations, the accent was harder to control. I wasn't sure whether the nerves created the accent or the accent created the nerves.

In grade three, I got so nervous about presenting my science project that I couldn't sleep the night before. When I talked to Mom about it, she suggested that dressing up might help me feel more confident.

I arrived at school the next day wearing khaki capri pants with a blouse and sandals instead of my usual T-shirt, shorts and running shoes. I think I even wore my hair loose instead of pulling it back into a ponytail or stuffing it under a baseball cap.

But it didn't make me feel more confident; it made me feel like I was pretending to be someone else.

Halfway through my presentation, the fire alarm went off. I felt so relieved as I marched across the schoolyard that I forgot I was wearing those stupid sandals instead of my running shoes. As soon as we were far enough from the building to see that it wasn't on fire, everyone in the class started running around the baseball field. As I turned to try and catch Sarah, I slipped on the wet grass and landed in the batter's box, which had been transformed by a spring shower into a huge mud puddle.

As soon as I stood up, I heard one of the boys shout, "Look! Bree's crapped in her capris!" The entire class rushed over to see. It seemed everyone in the class had something to say about my muddy bum.

And then, to my horror, the teacher made me finish my presentation when the fire drill was over. For the rest of the year, the chant *"Bree, Bree, crappy capri"* followed me through the playground. Just when I thought everyone had forgotten, someone would start the chant again. I hadn't heard it for a while, but I sure didn't want to give anyone another reason to make up a stupid rhyme about me.

Even so, Sarah still couldn't understand why I was so anxious about the presentation I had to give to the council. Nothing made Sarah nervous, because she truly didn't care what other people thought of her. I wished I could be more like that.

Sarah said I would feel better if I was well-prepared. So I did some research. I googled tree climbing and found a cool website for a group called TCI, which stands for Tree Climbers International. I found out that tree climbing is an actual sport that people compete in all over the world. And that lots of other people—including adults—think it's an awesome recreational activity. The website had tons of pictures of kids using ropes, harnesses and helmets to move from tree to tree up in the canopy. How cool is that?

The TCI website also had lots of great information about tree-climbing classes and a climber finder, so you could find a place to climb and even a buddy to climb with. But there was nothing about tree-climbing bylaws and how to have them overturned. I'd have to figure that out on my own.

Sarah and I also came up with the idea of interviewing the other kids in Cedar Grove so I could prove that I wasn't the only one upset about the bylaw. Unfortunately, this didn't get me very far either.

The first person I talked to was Ashley, the unofficial leader of the Cedar Grove Girly-Girls.

"So what do you think of this new bylaw?" I asked her.

"What bylaw?"

"You know. The new one that makes it illegal to climb trees in Cedar Grove."

"Oh, that," Ashley said as she straightened her pink dress. "I guess the Neighborhood Council thinks that tree climbing is dangerous."

"But what do YOU think?"

"Well, they would know. So I guess I agree. Tree climbing is dangerous."

"So you have no problem with all these restrictive new bylaws that the council keeps passing?"

"No, not really, Bree." She fiddled with one of the fancy clips in her hair. "I don't think there can be too many bylaws. Bylaws are important when so many people live so close together."

I was stunned into silence. Had Ashley been talking to my mom? That was totally something she would say.

"Sorry, Bree, but if you don't have any other questions I should go. It's skipping time."

"Oh, yeah, of course." Wasn't it always skipping time? "Have fun!" Somehow I managed to say this without rolling my eyes.

The next person I ran into was Ethan. He was sitting on the small patch of grass in front of his town-house, reading a book.

"What's up, Ethan?" I asked as I plopped myself down on the grass next to him.

"Not much," he replied. That's when I spotted the Magic Bag. Ethan must have realized I was looking at it, because he immediately tried to cover it with his book. But it was too late. I forgot all about my original line of questioning.

"So…how come you're not playing catch? Or street hockey?"

"Well," Ethan said slowly, refusing to look me in the eye, "I have to read this book…you know, for school."

"They make you read *A Brief History of Time* in grade four?"

Ethan's face turned bright red. "Well, they don't *make* you read it, but I kind of wanted to."

"Come on, Ethan, tell me what's going on. What's with the Magic Bag?" I asked, pointing to it.

"Oh, it's just a relaxation thing." Ethan picked up the bag and tossed it over to me. "Want to try it?"

"No." I tossed it back. Ethan winced as he caught it.

"I don't believe you, Ethan. Why were you holding it on your elbow the other day? And why wouldn't your mom let you play ball?"

"Oh, you know my mom. She's always worrying about something."

"What exactly was she worried about?" I asked. This was like trying to get information out of the mime at the Granville Island Public Market.

"Well, I kind of hurt my elbow."

"Duh. I figured that out already. The question is, why is it such a big secret?" Kids were always getting hurt. It was part of being a kid. And despite being a bit of a bookworm, Ethan was as active as the rest of us.

And then it hit me. "How did you hurt your elbow?"

"Um…I, uh, I fell," Ethan stammered.

"Fell how?"

"You know. I fell. From somewhere high to somewhere much lower. I landed on my elbow. But it's almost better."

"Did you fall from a tree, by any chance?"

"Maybe."

"Yes or no, Ethan."

"Yes," he said quietly.

I was silent for a minute. My brain needed time to catch up.

"Does anyone else know?" I finally asked.

"No," he replied. "And I really don't want them to find out. They already sort of blame me for all the new bylaws because my mom is president of the Neighborhood Council."

Ethan was right. It wasn't going to look good if kids found out that Ethan had been injured tree climbing. "Did your fall have anything to do with the new bylaw?"

"I honestly don't know. But Mom was pretty worried when she found out how far I had fallen. She took me to the hospital for X-rays and everything. There was a council meeting that night. The notice about the bylaw came out a few days later."

We sat in silence for a few minutes.

"Well, I'm glad you weren't hurt too badly," I said. "And don't worry, I won't tell anyone."

"Really?"

"Really."

"Thanks, Bree."

And that was the end of my interviews.

Chapter 5

By the time Tuesday evening finally arrived, I was a nervous wreck. I could hardly eat dinner even though Dad made his famous portobello mushroom burgers. I just nibbled on the bun until Mom told me I'd better get going. My butt felt like it was glued to the chair. I really didn't want to go. But I didn't want to be late either. Late would be bad.

"Good luck, Bree," Dad said as he walked me to the front door. "I wish I could come with you. If it was any other time of year—"

"I know," I said, cutting him off. "It's okay, Dad."

I knew even before I'd asked Dad to come to the meeting that he'd probably have a game to go to.

It was almost the trade deadline, a busy time for hockey scouts in the NHL. Mom had volunteered to come in his place, but I said no because I was worried she might make me even more nervous.

The smell of barbecued mushrooms was still floating in the air as I walked over to the common room at the far end of our complex. It made me feel a little better, so I tried to think about other happy things. Happy summer things like barbecuing and picnics at the beach. The days were starting to get longer and the rain was getting a little less cold. Spring in Vancouver lasted forever. But summer was coming. And I wanted to be able to climb trees!

Ms. Matheson greeted me at the door. "Good evening, Brianna," she said. "Glad you made it."

"Of course," I said as if it were no big deal. Just another council meeting!

"Your item is second on the agenda. You'll have to sit through the start of the meeting."

"Okay," I replied. Ms. Matheson waved me toward a chair at the big long table in the middle of the room. I sat down hesitantly. Last time I was in this room we were celebrating Sammy's first birthday.

That was three years ago, just after the Ambrosia family had moved to Cedar Grove. Sammy was just a baby, and supercute, but his older sister, Salina, couldn't stand him. So I treated him like he was my little brother, which was great because I'd always wanted one. That's why it was me, not Salina, who decorated this room with balloons, toy cars, streamers and a great big *HAPPY BIRTHDAY* banner.

Now the room looked very cold and businesslike.

"Let's get started," Ms. Matheson said, addressing the six council members who were standing around in little clusters. Probably chatting about the price of gas, their kids' report cards, how bad it is to put plastic in the microwave…you know—the weird stuff grown-ups care about.

"I now call this meeting to order. Thank you for coming," Ms. Matheson said once everyone was seated. "We'll begin with the formalities."

There was a bunch of chatter about motions and minutes. I was too nervous to pay attention, but I dutifully turned my head in the direction of whoever was speaking. I recognized a couple of the other parents, which made me wish that Mom had insisted on coming.

After a lot of back and forth, Ms. Matheson finally said, "Let's get started." She turned toward the opposite end of the table, where Mrs. Leary sat. I hadn't noticed her until that moment. She's Cedar Grove's oldest and grouchiest resident. She lives next door to Tyler. I was glad she didn't live next to me.

"The first item on the agenda has been brought forward by Noreen Leary, Unit 31." Ms. Matheson looked at her and said, "Please be brief, Mrs. Leary."

Mrs. Leary cleared her throat. "Well, thank you in advance for hearing me out," she said slowly. I sank down into my chair, grateful for the opportunity to observe for a while.

"I've come here tonight to ask the council to consider implementing a new bylaw." Even though no one made a sound, I could feel the room groan as Mrs. Leary said this. She went on. "It's about pets. I am sick and tired of cleaning up doggie doo-doo in my backyard."

Laughter tickled the back of my throat when I heard Mrs. Leary say *doo-doo*. I had to suck in my cheeks, hard, to prevent the laughter from erupting. I knew that laughing at a council meeting would be bad. It was just so funny to hear a woman who must be close to a hundred talk about dog poo. Even funnier was the fact that everyone else at the meeting seemed to be taking her so seriously.

"What exactly are you proposing?" Ms. Matheson asked.

"There should be a limit on how many pets are allowed per unit."

No one said anything. Mr. Morrow, Michael's dad, was busy scribbling notes. He'd been writing since the meeting began.

"Or maybe there should be no pets at all," Mrs. Leary said, looking around the room.

"But you have three cats!" Debra Williams exclaimed. Mrs. Williams was Ashley's mom. They had a poodle named Puddles.

"Oh, I'm not talking about cats. I'm talking about other pests. I mean, *pets*." Mrs. Leary looked a bit flustered. I sucked in my cheeks again, but this time I couldn't stop the corners of my lips from moving upward. This was too funny! I couldn't wait to tell Sarah!

"But cats are pets."

"I mean dogs! They are the ones that are making doo-doo all over my lawn!"

"So," Ms. Matheson said slowly, "you would like to propose a bylaw that limits the number of dogs per unit?"

"Yes! Limit the number of dogs. Or ban them altogether. That would take care of the doo-doo and the barking. Sometimes the barking keeps me up at night."

"All right, Mrs. Leary, I think the council understands your concerns. We will discuss the matter further. Thank you for coming." Ms. Matheson said this quite firmly, using what was probably her best principal voice.

Mrs. Leary persisted. "But really, we need more bylaws. And we need to increase the fines given to Cedar Grove residents who break the rules."

"We already have the highest fines allowed by the Neighborhood Act," Mrs. Williams said.

"It's two fifty for the first infraction and five twenty-five for the second. Units in debt to the Cedar Grove Neighborhood Corporation can be forced into foreclosure," said one of the council members who had been silent until now. "That's a pretty stiff penalty, if you ask me."

I didn't understand all that, but it sounded similar to what Ethan had said. He's a smart guy.

"Well, something more has to be done." Mrs. Leary didn't seem to understand either.

"As I said, we'll discuss your concerns at a later date. Right now, we need to move on to the next item on our agenda."

Mrs. Leary frowned and then rose awkwardly from the table. I guess she realized that she had no choice. But she took forever putting on her coat and scarf and gloves. She had a ridiculous amount of clothing, considering the weather and the fact that she only had to walk a couple of steps to her front door.

When Mrs. Leary was finally gone, Ms. Matheson turned to me. "The second item on the agenda is in regard to interim bylaw 47.21. I'd like to introduce Brianna Bridges, Unit 83, who has asked for an opportunity to address the council on this matter."

My heart was suddenly racing. During Mrs. Leary's performance, I had forgotten why I was here. I wasn't ready for this!

My throat was dry. I didn't know what to do. Everyone was looking at me. "Do I need to stand up or something?" I asked, absentmindedly running my hand along the leg of my jeans. Even though my jeans were clean, the words *Bree, Bree, crappy capri* floated through my head.

"No, that won't be necessary, Brianna. Just speak loudly so everyone can hear what you have to say."

Speak loudly? I could hardly even breathe.

Chapter 6

I took a deep breath. And another. My heart felt like the Energizer Bunny's drum. Everyone was staring at me. I had to speak. Silence was bad.

I glanced at my notes.

1. *Tree climbing is good for kids because it is mentally stimulating. Finding your way up a tree is like solving a puzzle.*
2. *Tree climbing is good exercise. It provides a thorough workout for the arms, legs and spine. It also enhances flexibility and coordination.*
3. *There are all kinds of studies showing that kids are not getting enough exercise.*

4. *Parents like it when their kids climb trees because it is free. And they don't have to drive them anywhere.*

5. *Our principal, Mr. Lee, is always saying that kids need to spend more time outside appreciating nature.*

6. *You cannot climb trees inside.*

7. *Tree climbing is very safe.*

Some of these ideas came from the tree-climbing website. Some of them came from a brainstorming session I had with Sarah. I added the part about Mr. Lee to impress Ms. Matheson. I figured she was more likely to listen to another school principal than she was to me.

"Well, I, um…" My throat was really dry. I looked at Mrs. Leary's empty seat and said the first thing that came to mind. "Thank you for inviting me to come."

My heart was still thumping away. I was sure everyone in the room could hear it. But I went on anyway. "I'd like the council to reconsider the bylaw against tree climbing."

"Go on," Ms. Matheson prodded.

"I, well, I don't think it's necessary."

"The council created the bylaw because we felt that tree climbing was putting the children of Cedar Grove at risk." Ms. Matheson looked around the table as she said this.

This wasn't going the way I had hoped. I looked at my notes again. Then I took another deep breath and said, "But I would like you, and, um, the council to consider some of the many ways that tree climbing is a healthy activity for kids to be involved in." It was my turn to look around the table. To my surprise, some of the council members were nodding. Mr. Morrow was even smiling at me encouragingly.

That's when things started to get better. Eventually, my heart stopped pounding and I started breathing normally. I didn't follow my notes exactly. But I think I covered everything.

I went over the last point—tree climbing is safe— really quickly. Obviously, safety was the main issue. But I really didn't know how to convince the council that tree climbing wasn't dangerous. Except to compare it to something really, really dangerous like motorcycle racing or skydiving. But I didn't think it would be a good idea to start associating tree climbing with those kinds of sports.

After finding out about Ethan's fall, I'd done some more research online, specifically about safety. I'd found some conflicting information. Although there was nothing about townhouse complexes, I had learned that tree climbing was banned in a lot of school playgrounds across North America. There was even an interview with an American PTA member who described tree climbing as a "life threatening activity" responsible for over 140 deaths per year. I wasn't about to tell the council that.

The TCI website didn't have any useful suggestions on its safety page either. It just said stuff like, *Stay on a rope, wear the right gear, get training from a qualified instructor and never forget the fall.* Most of these suggestions didn't even apply to backyard tree climbing. I mean, the trees in Cedar Grove aren't that big. And I certainly wasn't going to talk about the fall. That would be bad.

I definitely didn't want Ms. Matheson to start thinking about Ethan's fall. I figured it would be game over if that happened. Truth was, although I'd had a few minor injuries from tree climbing, I'd never considered it dangerous. But what if Ethan had really been hurt? Would that have changed the way I felt about it? Could Ashley and everyone else be right about tree climbing—was it really that dangerous?

I was done in less than five minutes, but it felt like forever. When I finished talking, Ms. Matheson thanked me again for coming. "We'll take your points into consideration."

"But…" I felt like things weren't complete, like I needed to say more. I wanted to scream, *It's not fair! I love climbing trees. I'm not a grouchy old lady like Mrs. Leary! Please take me seriously!*

"I'm afraid I'm going to have to ask you to leave now, Brianna"—Ms. Matheson frowned at me—"so we can get on with the rest of the meeting."

"But what about the bylaw? Can it be overturned?" I wasn't feeling nervous anymore. Not at all. Just desperate for the council to see things my way.

"As I said before, the bylaw was put in place because the council thinks that tree climbing is putting the children of Cedar Grove at risk. We chose not to delay the decision until the Annual General Meeting because we're worried that someone will get hurt trying to climb as high and as far as you do. You do not set the best example, Brianna." Ms. Matheson stopped suddenly and glanced at the other council members. Then she continued, "There will be further discussion based on your input. We will let you know when a decision has been made."

I didn't say anything as I stood up to leave. I heard mumbling around the table about the AGM and ratification, but I was too upset to really listen.

You do not set the best example, Brianna. Ms. Matheson's words turned my desperation into a pot of anger that was dangerously close to boiling over.

It wasn't fair. Kids have to put up with too many rules. I was sick of the Cedar Grove Neighborhood Council and their stupid bylaws.

Chapter 7

A couple of days after the meeting, I came home from school to find Tyler and Michael playing basketball in front of Tyler's garage. I tried to walk by quickly, but there was really no way to avoid them. I couldn't reach the front door of my house without walking right under their net.

As soon as he saw me, Tyler said, "Did you hear the news, Bree?" He had a big smirk on his face.

"They're finally going to fumigate your townhouse? To get rid of the big creepy bug that's pestering the good people of Cedar Grove?"

"Funny." Tyler wasn't laughing, but I heard Michael chuckle. "Your meeting with the council was a waste of time, Bree. They're not changing the tree-climbing bylaw."

"What? How do you know?" I felt my cheeks flush with anger.

"I've got my sources," Tyler said smugly.

"Sorry, Bree," said a voice behind me. I turned and saw Ethan sitting on his front steps. He was still on the sidelines. I looked at his hurt elbow, even though I knew there was nothing to see.

"It's true?" I asked him.

"Mom said that the council took your arguments into consideration, but the interim bylaw remains in effect."

"Interim?" I couldn't understand why everyone kept using that word. Wasn't a bylaw just a bylaw?

"It has be called an interim bylaw until it gets voted on and passed at the AGM."

"Did your mom tell you why they couldn't just overturn it?"

"She wouldn't go into detail, but I think there might be legal issues," Ethan said.

"Who cares about legal issues? We're kids. We should be able to climb trees!" I snapped.

"The council has to care about legal issues and they still think tree climbing is dangerous."

"But it's not!"

I had been thinking a lot about safety since my presentation. I knew I hadn't done a good job convincing the council that tree climbing was safe. I guess Ethan's injury and the stuff I'd found on the Internet had momentarily given me some doubts.

"Tree climbing is no more dangerous than basketball," I said, pointing at the net. "Any sport is dangerous if you don't do it properly."

I was certain of my argument now, but unfortunately, I was using it on Ethan, who was only trying to be helpful. I was just so mad at myself for not making a stronger case to the Neighborhood Council.

Tyler and Michael were staring at me. "It doesn't really matter whether it's dangerous or not," Tyler said calmly. "Point is, there will never be tree climbing in Cedar Grove again. And it doesn't matter what you do. Give it up, Bree. You're not the boss around here."

"Neither are you!" I stared back at Tyler and narrowed my eyes. "And this means you can't climb either."

"So what?" Tyler shrugged and took a shot at the net. The basketball swished through the hoop. "There are other things to do."

"But you can't climb trees," I repeated.

"The monkey bars at the playground are pretty good," Michael said.

"But that's not good enough for little Brianna," Tyler said in a silly crybaby voice.

"You're just jealous because you're not as good a climber as me!" I spit the words at him. I could feel the back of my throat start to burn and I bit my cheeks to hold back the tears.

"Me? Jealous of you? Before the council destroyed the jungle gym, I beat you in every climbing competition we ever had."

"You've never beat me up a tree!" I shot back.

I saw him wince briefly. Then he wound up and fired at me again. "I certainly beat you on the pitcher's mound."

It was my turn to wince. The competition between Tyler and me started in the spring of grade four when we'd both tried out to pitch for the Bulldogs, our local Little League baseball team. We were pretty evenly matched back then, so it took the Bulldogs' coach all preseason to select the starting pitcher. Losing out to Tyler hadn't bothered me much back then. I was just happy to be part of the team. But Tyler was upset even though he'd won. Dad said it was because a girl who was almost a full year younger than him had come so close to stealing his position. All I know is that the rivalry between us had been fierce ever since.

"Why do you like climbing trees so much anyway, Bree?" Ethan asked, probably hoping to end the fight between Tyler and me. Everyone knows Ethan is a kid who doesn't like conflict.

I took a few breaths to calm myself down. Crying would be bad. "It's fun," I said as I looked up, "and it makes me feel free." As much as I liked playing with all the other kids in Cedar Grove, sometimes I liked to get away from them too. Up in the trees I could be alone. In my own little world.

"Well, say goodbye to freedom, Bree," Tyler said, snapping me back to reality.

"Come on, Tyler," Michael said, bouncing the basketball. "Let's finish this game."

Michael isn't sensitive like Ethan. But I noticed that he sometimes got caught between pleasing Tyler and saying what he really wanted to say. Honestly, I wondered why Michael put up with Tyler at all.

Tyler turned toward the net and took a pass from Michael. I gave Ethan an apologetic smile even though I was still angry. This whole mess wasn't his fault.

Without saying goodbye, I headed over to the big collection of metal mailboxes that line the entry to Cedar Grove. I opened up our little slot with the key I'd convinced Mom to give me since she was never home early enough to get the mail herself. I pulled out a stack of envelopes and flyers, instantly spotting the notice from the Cedar Grove Neighborhood Council even though it was at the bottom of the pile. No one else used paper the color of pee.

I didn't unfold the notice until Dad came home. I was afraid to read it. I didn't want Tyler and Ethan's story confirmed.

When Dad handed me the notice I was ready to be disappointed. But I wasn't prepared for another shock.

Dear Resident of Cedar Grove,
This notice is to serve as a reminder of Cedar Grove bylaw 5.12.

Bylaw 5.12: A pet owner must ensure that a permitted pet is kept quiet, controlled and clean. Any excrement on common property must be immediately disposed of by the person supervising the pet.

The Neighborhood Council appreciates the effort of each individual resident in making Cedar Grove a clean and pleasant place to live. Sincerely,
Cedar Grove Neighborhood Council

The Council had listened to Mrs. Leary! They'd even sent out a notice. But they had totally ignored me. They weren't even considerate enough to inform me of their decision. I only knew the neighborhood council wasn't changing the tree-climbing bylaw because Marion Matheson had blabbed to her son. And Ethan had spread the news to everyone, including Tyler.

I crumpled the notice into a ball and threw it toward Dad, who was flipping through the rest of the mail.

"I hate Cedar Grove!" I growled.

"I'm sorry, Bree," Dad said. I could barely hear him through the rush of blood to my head. I was too angry to answer. I stomped up to my room, hoping that everyone in the townhouse complex could hear each step.

Chapter 8

I wasn't about to give up. But I wasn't going to the Neighborhood Council again. What a waste of time. I had to come up with a better idea.

According to Mom, I always had two choices: follow the rules or change them. If tree climbing was dangerous, then I should stop doing it and find a new hobby like reading or skipping. If tree climbing wasn't dangerous, I needed to prove it to the council. When I reminded Mom that I'd tried, she asked if I really believed that was true. She said this nicely, but her raised eyebrows told me otherwise.

Dad kept telling me there would be other trees to climb. He said he would take us on a big camping trip in the summer. Somewhere up past Whistler, where there are tons of trees in every shape and size. "They'll be perfect for climbing," he promised and then added, "as long as a bear doesn't get there first." As soon as I heard that, I knew Mom would never let us go.

Sarah thought I should ignore the bylaw and climb the trees in Cedar Grove. "Just don't let them catch you." Sarah could get away with doing things like that. Not me. I had one of those faces that everyone could read like a book. The minute I climbed a tree, everyone would know it.

A better idea finally came to me two weeks later. I was sitting in class, trying not to be distracted by the sun streaming in through the window above my desk. The days were getting longer and longer, and it was finally warm enough to shed some layers of Gore-Tex and Polarfleece. Short sleeves would come next. I couldn't imagine summer without tree climbing in Cedar Grove.

Our social studies teacher, Mr. Vandermeer, was talking about Clayoquot Sound, an area on Vancouver Island that's famous for its old-growth trees. The pictures of the trees were interesting (they had massive trunks that looked as if they would be difficult to climb) and so was the story of a huge protest that happened there in 1993.

In one picture a group of people were standing around a small pickup truck parked across a dirt road. In the background I could see huge trucks and other tree-destroying machines. According to Mr. Vandermeer, some of the protesters actually chained themselves to the trees to stop those machines from doing their work.

My mind started to wander again as I imagined being part of something so radical. Each person in that picture looked so ordinary. But each one cared enough about the trees to stand up to the big rich forestry companies that were cutting them down. Working together, the protestors had found a way to have their voices heard.

"Can you guess how many people were arrested?" When Mr. Vandermeer's voice changed, I snapped back to attention. I knew he had asked a question. Everyone was silent.

"Brianna?" Mr. Vandermeer asked.

"Um, ten?" I guessed, thinking again about the people in the picture.

Mr. Vandermeer laughed. No one else did though, so I knew my answer hadn't been totally stupid. "Almost a thousand," he exclaimed, spreading his arms wide so that everyone would understand what a big deal this was, "even though the activists were protesting peacefully."

Mr. Vandermeer showed more pictures. There were tons of people carrying signs that said things like *Ban Old-Growth Logging*, *Save the Ancient Forests* and *Clear-Cutting Kills*.

"In the end, the protestors were successful. Premier Michael Harcourt's decision to allow logging in Clayoquot Sound was overturned. To this day, the Clayoquot Sound protest is considered a major victory for the environmental movement." The bell rang just as Mr. Vandermeer finished with his slide show. He was still talking, but no one heard the end of the story.

That's when the idea hit me.

I caught up with Sarah as every student in the class tried to jam through the door at the same time. "I think I've got it!"

"Got what?" Sarah asked.

"I'm going to organize a protest."

"Clayoquot Sound has already been saved." Sarah ran her tongue over her braces and reached into her bag for a granola bar. "Weren't you listening?"

"No, not Clayoquot Sound. Cedar Grove, silly," I said.

Sarah stared at me as she ripped open her snack.

"I'll get all the kids of Cedar Grove together to protest the tree-climbing bylaw!" I didn't wait for Sarah's response. I just waved my hand in her direction as I sprinted toward home. I couldn't wait to get my protest started.

Chapter 9

"I now call this meeting to order. Thank you for coming," I said, doing my best impression of Ms. Matheson, Neighborhood Council President. I looked around. There were at least twelve kids sitting on the grassy hill behind Cedar Grove. No one was paying much attention to me though. They were all too busy munching on gummy worms. News about the meeting had spread fast thanks to my promise to provide candy.

Even Tyler was there, probably just to make sure no one listened to what I had to say. Of course that didn't stop him from chowing down on all the goodies Dad had picked up for me at Costco.

"As I'm sure you know," I continued, "tree climbing is now illegal in Cedar Grove."

I waited for a response. Everyone just looked at me. Then Sarah shouted, "Boo! Hiss!"

I'd brought Sarah along for support, even though she doesn't live in Cedar Grove. I was pretty sure Tyler liked her. And I suspected she might even like him back. Maybe not *like* like. But she didn't think he was as disgusting as I did.

Anyway, I was superglad Sarah was there. I hadn't thought I would need her help so soon. A couple of the older kids joined in on the booing and hissing. The younger ones started squirming around, their sweet tooths temporarily satisfied. Sammy chewed on a blade of grass.

"Exactly," I said over the noise. "It isn't fair, and I think we should do something about it."

"I thought you already tried, Bree," Tyler said.

"I met with the Neighborhood Council," I said slowly, "to let them know I didn't like the bylaw. But one voice is not enough. We have to speak out against this rule together."

"I think we should follow the rules." This came from Ashley. Surprise, surprise. Then she added, "Tree climbing is obviously dangerous."

"Besides," Tyler sneered, "you're the only one who cares about tree climbing, Bree."

I scanned the crowd for Peter. My stomach sank as I realized he wasn't there. And neither were any of the other kids who really liked to climb trees.

I took a deep breath and went on, ignoring Tyler's comment. "Tree climbing is no more dangerous than basketball," I said, looking directly at Tyler because basketball was his sport. "What if they ban that next?"

"They would never ban basketball," Tyler replied.

"They might if someone got hurt," I said. "And what about street hockey? Kids get hurt playing street hockey all the time. And Mrs. Leary is always screaming that someone's going to break her window."

A look of fear crept into Michael's eyes. It was enough to make me hopeful that my strategy just might work. I needed to make everyone realize that the next bylaw could take away their favorite thing.

"The Neighborhood Council would never ban street hockey," Tyler said. The squirming had stopped. Everyone was listening now.

"The Neighborhood Council just keeps passing more bylaws," I said. "They've taken away the jungle gym, the weight room, the storage locker, the parking garage, and now they've taken our trees. We have to stop them before it gets any more out of control."

"Nothing's out of control," said Ashley. "The council is just trying to make sure we are safe."

"What's next?" I went on. "Skipping?"

"Why would anyone ban skipping?" Salina, one of the Cedar Grove Girly-Girls, asked.

"It's loud. It's dangerous. Someone could trip over the rope and break something."

"You're blowing this out of proportion," Ashley said. "They would never go that far."

"How do you know how far they will go?" I looked her straight in the eye and pulled out my ace. "When I was at the council meeting they were talking about banning dogs."

Ashley gasped. A couple of the other kids looked at me in alarm.

"We have to let them know that they can't ban everything. We have to take a stand. Starting now. Starting with the tree-climbing bylaw."

"How?" Ethan asked.

"We need to organize a protest," I said.

"A protest?" Tyler looked surprised.

"*Pro-test. Pro-test. Pro-test*," Sarah chanted.

"This Saturday"—I raised my voice—"we'll march through Cedar Grove." Some of the kids nodded, so I decided to say something inspirational. Something I'd read on one of the protest signs in Mr. Vandermeer's lesson on Clayoquot Sound. "Together we can make a difference!" I yelled.

"The Neighborhood Council won't care. They'll just think we're playing some silly game." Tyler again.

"*Pro-test. Pro-test. Pro-test*," Sarah was still chanting.

"We'll sing songs. We'll make signs. We'll make sure that everyone knows how we feel!" I hoped my enthusiasm was catching on.

"Sounds like fun," Salina said. "I like marching and singing."

"Good! You'll be in charge of songs." I really hoped she wasn't going to suggest skipping rhymes.

"But I don't know any protest songs."

"They don't need to be protest songs; we just need to make noise"—I waved my hand toward Sarah—"like Sarah is doing now."

"*Pro-test. Pro-test. Pro-test*," Sarah continued, louder than ever.

"I'll help. We're good at making noise," Ashley said, gesturing toward the other Cedar Grove Girly-Girls.

"And I'm good with signs," said Michael, ignoring Tyler's glare. "I always help my Mom with her protest stuff. I think the signs we made for *Mother's Against the Metric System* are still in the garage."

"Awesome! Michael, you get a group together to make signs." If Michael was on board, this protest might actually happen! But I still needed Tyler. Everyone listened to him.

"This is stupid." Tyler scowled.

Sarah increased the volume again. "*Pro-test. Pro-test. Pro-test…*"

"I think we should have snacks," Ashley suggested.

"Okay. You do snacks," I said, even though I didn't think it was necessary.

"How about drums?" Salina asked.

"Drums?"

"Yeah, you know, to help make noise."

"Oh, sure, drums would be great." I hadn't thought of that.

"I'll bring some of Sammy's toy instruments."

"Good idea," I said. "If anyone has anything that can be used to make noise bring it along."

Sarah changed the chant. "*No more rules! No more rules!*" Some of the other kids joined in. The momentum was definitely building.

But then Tyler spoke up again. "It's never going to work," he said, dashing my hope that this was going to be easy. Some heads nodded in agreement. If Tyler wasn't going to join the protest, I was in trouble. "Why would the council listen?"

Sarah stopped chanting. "They can't listen if you don't say anything."

As Tyler turned toward Sarah, the scowl on his face suddenly disappeared.

"You have to make them listen," Sarah continued.

"She's right. We have to do something! Before they ban hockey," Michael said.

"Or pets!" Ashley added.

"But how do we make them listen?" Tyler asked. The challenge was gone from his voice. He was almost smiling.

"You protest," Sarah said. "Loudly."

"It's not enough. We have to do more," Tyler said.

"Like what?" asked Michael.

I thought. Hard. But as much as I wanted to have an answer, I couldn't come up with one on the spot. I thought about the Clayoquot Sound protestors blocking the tree-destroying machines. Physically stopping them from clear-cutting the old-growth trees. Tyler was right; we needed some kind of leverage.

There was a long pause. Everyone looked at each other anxiously.

It was Tyler who broke the silence. He surprised us all, but mostly me, by answering his own question. "None of us will take a bath until they change the bylaw."

There was silence again while everyone thought this over.

"Can we shower?" Ashley finally asked.

"No. We get dirtier and dirtier until they are forced to listen."

"I'm not sure I like that idea…" Ashley frowned.

"Yippee! No bath!" Sammy shouted as he threw a big handful of grass in the air.

"But my Mom will just make me bathe." Ethan looked worried.

"She can't *make* you do anything," Tyler said firmly.

"Yeah. You can't force someone to take a bath," Michael said, doing his best to get back on Tyler's good side.

Ethan looked doubtful, and I kind of had to agree with him—his mom probably could make him take a bath.

"*No trees, no bath! No trees, no bath!*" Sarah chanted. Michael joined in. Sammy and his sister joined in. Soon everyone was chanting, even Ashley. My strategy had worked!

I smiled at Tyler and started chanting too. Tyler didn't smile back. He was still looking at Sarah as his voice joined the others. "*No trees, no bath! No trees, no bath!*"

We had ourselves a protest.

Chapter 10

"*No trees, no bath! No trees, no bath! No trees, no bath!*" There were over twenty of us chanting and marching in unison. Almost every kid in Cedar Grove had come out to protest the tree-climbing bylaw—and some of them, like Peter, hadn't even been at the meeting. A few of them even brought friends. Sarah was at the front helping the Cedar Grove Girly-Girls lead the chant. Not that we needed any help.

We were loud.

We were also very visible.

Michael had found a bunch of picket signs in his garage. The night before, we'd covered the old blue and white slogans and replaced them with our own.

The new signs read, *Trees are meant for climbing* and *If we can't climb, we won't bathe* and *No More Rules*. On Michael's sign, he'd written the word *RULES* in the middle of a big red circle with a line through it. Like the No Smoking signs you see all over the place. Tyler's sign was the same except that, instead of *RULES,* he'd drawn a bathtub in the middle of the circle. He was really into the no-bathing thing.

On my sign the words *Need to be free to climb a tree* were written in bright green. I held it high and marched at the back, making sure everyone stayed in line. Cedar Grove isn't very big, so we made the same loop over and over again.

It wasn't long before we started to get some attention.

Mrs. Leary leaned out her window and yelled, "I can't hear *Coronation Street*!" Then she added, "There are bylaws in Cedar Grove, you know!" Of course, that made us all laugh. She obviously had no idea what we were doing. Poor old Mrs. Leary. Had she ever been a kid? It was hard to imagine. We moved quickly past her house.

Dad stood at the corner with a couple of the other parents, drinking coffee. He smiled as we marched by. When I'd told him about the tree-climbing protest, he'd gone on and on about how proud he was of me and about how much he'd admired the hippie protesters he grew up with. He always wanted to join them, but he never had the time to do anything but play hockey.

Mom wasn't exactly supportive of the protest, but she said it was good that I was doing something. Lucky for me, she was at an engineering conference, so I didn't have to deal with her disapproval.

Our message was obviously being heard by some residents of Cedar Grove, but I hadn't seen Ms. Matheson or anyone else I recognized from the Neighborhood Council. I started getting a little anxious. I'd been so busy planning the protest that I hadn't really thought about the possibility that it might not work. It had to work.

After an hour we stopped and had some snacks. Cookies and juice supplied by Mrs. Williams. It seemed strange that she was supporting us, given that she was a member of the council. Was it possible that she was afraid Mrs. Leary could convince the council to ban pets? Whatever the reason, I was glad Ashley had suggested snacks. Protesting was tiring.

It was hard to get everyone going again after the break. Some of the kids had had enough.

But then Sarah and Ethan started chanting, "*We want to climb! We want to climb! We want to climb!*"

Sammy and Salina brought out a bunch of noise-makers—toy drums and maracas and a tambourine. Tyler and Michael started banging on metal garbage lids with hockey sticks. Soon everyone was marching again, and we were louder than ever.

We must have passed Ethan's house about a hundred times. I'd almost given up hope when Ms. Matheson suddenly appeared on the doorstop. "Okay," she shouted above the noise, "what's it going to take to make you stop?"

Almost immediately, everyone stopped marching, chanting, rattling and banging.

Knowing that she had our full attention, Ms. Matheson used her principal's voice to say, "This kind of behavior is not acceptable." She glared at Tyler, who just happened to be standing right in front of her.

"It was Bree's idea," Tyler said. Coward, I thought.

"Brianna?" Ms. Matheson said, rubbing her forehead. "What's this all about?"

"We're protesting the Cedar Grove bylaw against tree climbing," I said, trying to sound confident and official.

"What you are doing," Ms. Matheson said, still rubbing her forehead, "is disturbing everyone."

"It's a peaceful protest, Ms. Matheson," I said. "We want to make sure everyone in Cedar Grove knows how we feel."

"I think everyone has heard you loud and clear." As Ms. Matheson said this, she scanned the group, trying to make eye contact. A principal trick, for sure. Poor Ethan. "Now why don't you use those hockey sticks the way they are meant to be used," she said to Tyler and Michael.

"We're not done protesting, ma'am," Michael responded.

"How long do you plan to go on?" Ms. Matheson asked. She glanced at the other parents. There was a big group of them now. Dad had brought out a bunch of lawn chairs and set them up in front of our garage. They were drinking coffee and eating Timbits.

They were acting like we were entertainment. I wasn't sure if that was a good thing or not.

"We're not bathing until the bylaw is changed," Tyler said, confident now that Michael and I had spoken up. "Or showering," he added. Just to be clear, I guess.

"Good luck with that," Ms. Matheson said sharply. She turned around and closed the front door behind her. Ethan stood trembling next to Sarah.

"Now they'll probably make a bylaw against protests," someone said. Everyone laughed, but it was nervous laughter.

We marched a little more, this time chanting, "*No more rules! No more rules!*" But the protest didn't last much longer. The enthusiasm was gone.

I should have known that was a sign of things to come.

Chapter 11

At first, the no-bathing thing was no big deal. But on day five I started to feel dirty and discouraged. After social studies, I stayed behind to ask Mr. Vandermeer how long they'd protested in Clayoquot Sound before the clear-cutting stopped. Mr. Vandermeer laughed and said, "Years." I didn't think that was very funny. There was no way I could go years without climbing or taking a bath.

When I got home from school, Tyler and Michael were out playing basketball. They asked if I wanted to shoot some hoops with them. I couldn't climb trees, which is what I really wanted to do, and I wasn't about to start skipping or reading, so I decided to join them.

Bad idea. I got my first whiff of BO as I tried to block one of Tyler's shots. He ended up scoring on me because I was gasping for breath. What a smell! Michael wasn't quite as bad but he still stunk. Boys are so disgusting.

"PEEUW!" I yelled after a few more minutes of torture. I couldn't take it anymore.

"What's your problem?" Tyler asked as he sank another layup.

"You stink."

"Duh," said Tyler. "What did you think was going to happen when we stopped bathing? That's the whole point. Our 'stink,' as you call it, is what forces our parents and the Council to take action and change the bylaw." He obviously wasn't bothered by it at all.

Michael, on the other hand, looked a bit self-conscious. "At least that's the theory," he said as he passed me the ball.

"Well, you've forced *me* to take action. I'm outta here." I passed the ball back to Michael and headed home to get my bike.

I needed some space. As I rode, I managed to clear my head and not think about anything. It was great. I felt better than I had in days. No, weeks.

Maybe months. It felt like I'd been fighting this tree-climbing bylaw forever.

But the good feeling disappeared as soon as I returned to Cedar Grove and ran into Ashley. She was out walking Puddles, her poodle. I knew right away that she'd taken a bath or a shower more recently than me. Her pretty blond hair was bouncing around her shoulders, so clean it almost sparkled.

"Hi, Bree!" she called out enthusiastically.

"Hey," I mumbled. I didn't want to stop, but it didn't look like I had a choice. She was blocking my path, and Puddles had decided it was time for a little "doo-doo," as Mrs. Leary called it.

"Bike ride?" she said as she pulled out a bag to clean up the poo.

I wanted to scream. I was on my bike, wearing my helmet. Of course I was out for a bike ride! I would be riding right now if her clean body wasn't in my way! With as much self-control as I could muster, I shot back, "Dog walk?"

Ashley laughed as she bent over to fill the bag. "I don't want to break the rules!" She held the bag up proudly so I could take a good look. Yuck.

"What about the protest?" I asked when the bag was finally out of my face.

"What do you mean?"

"The protest? No bathing?"

"Oh." She looked down. "That."

"Well?" I demanded.

"Well," she said slowly, "I didn't think we were really serious about that."

"Not serious? Do you want the council to prevent Cedar Grove residents from owning pets?"

"No. Of course not." Ashley looked at Puddles. "I want the council to stop making unnecessary new bylaws as much as you do. But the no-bathing thing... I just thought it was a gimmick."

"Yes! A gimmick to try and force the council to listen," I said with disgust. "And to be effective, we all need to do it. When the council members see you looking all sparkly clean, they aren't going to take us seriously at all!"

"And you think that not bathing is going to make them take us seriously? I think it makes us look like silly little kids who are mad because we're not getting our way."

"And I think you just couldn't handle being dirty. So much for solidarity."

"I'm sorry you feel that way, Brianna." Ashley didn't seem angry. Just truly sad that we had a difference of opinion. Again.

"Well, me too." The back of my throat was starting to burn. With my teeth clenched I opened my mouth just wide enough to say, "I better get home."

"Me too. See you around." She gave her dog a pat on the head and started to lead her away.

I rode in the opposite direction, toward the mailboxes. Mrs. Leary was already there, fumbling to find her tiny mailbox key on a ring that looked like it belonged to the school janitor. She must have kept every key from every car and house she'd ever owned.

I waited, trying to be patient. It had been almost a week since the protest, and I hadn't heard anything from the Neighborhood Council. I kept thinking I'd see one of their pee-colored notices in the mail, but nothing had showed up yet.

When Mrs. Leary was finally finished, she turned and looked me right in the eye without saying a word. Then she kind of scrunched her nose and limped away.

This was typical Mrs. Leary, but it still made me panic. What if I smelled as bad as Tyler or Michael?

Thank goodness it was almost the weekend. I didn't want to deal with people anymore. And I really didn't want my classmates to start noticing my lack of hygiene. That would be bad.

When I finally opened our mailbox, I spotted the notice right away. My hands were trembling as I rushed to unfold the paper. I was positive that our protest had finally been successful.

But the notice had nothing to do with tree climbing. It was another reminder about cleaning up dog poo! This time threatening to fine anyone who was caught not cleaning up after their dog. What were they planning? To do DNA testing to determine which dog the poo belonged to?

Well, score two for Mrs. Leary and none for me. Now I was even more discouraged.

How long could our protest go on? Was anyone even listening? They were treating us like a bunch of kids who didn't matter. But we had something to say! And it was just as important as Mrs. Leary's constant complaints.

This was so unfair!

Chapter 12

I spent most of the weekend feeling sorry for myself. It was raining and I couldn't climb, so I just stayed inside, feeling miserable and dirty.

On Sunday afternoon, I finally forced myself to go outside and find someone to play with. The sun had won its battle with the clouds, and I was starting to feel pathetic.

I found Ethan sitting under a big cherry tree in full bloom. He was reading again.

I sat down next to him. Right away I could smell soap. I sniffed the air to make sure it wasn't just the cherry blossoms. Nope, definitely soap.

I didn't want another confrontation like the one I'd had with Ashley. Ethan was my friend. But I needed to know what was going on.

"So," I started gently, "what're you reading now?"

"*The Collected Papers of Albert Einstein*," he said, without looking up.

I waited a minute, wondering if he was going to stop reading. This was weird. Ethan was normally excited to see me.

"So," I began again when it was clear that my silent strategy wasn't working, "how do you think the protest is going?"

Ethan sighed and closed his book. "Don't be mad, Bree."

"What?" I asked, trying to sound innocent.

"Mom made me take a bath. For Church. It's Palm Sunday, you know."

"Oh." My parents never took me to church. Mom said she was more spiritual than religious, and Dad said he just wasn't interested.

"I really had no choice, Bree." Ethan looked sad enough to cry.

"I know," I replied. I couldn't imagine what it was like to have Ms. Matheson as a mother, but I wasn't surprised that she had forced Ethan into bathing. Really, it was more surprising that he'd lasted this long.

"So, what now?"

"I don't know, Ethan. It's not looking good."

"No, it's not."

"As long as you are clean, your mom isn't going to care that the rest of us are dirty and smelly."

"There are other parents on the council who might care," Ethan said hopefully.

"Maybe."

We were both silent for a while.

"How's your elbow?" I asked finally.

"Oh, it's totally fine now," said Ethan, stretching his arm out to demonstrate.

"I'm glad. Was it a really bad fall?"

"No. Not really. It was Mom's reaction that was bad."

"Yeah," I said. "Does it make you think tree climbing is dangerous?"

"No." Ethan didn't even hesitate as he said this. "It was my own fault. I should have been more careful."

"So you'd like to be able to climb trees again?"

"Yes! I'd love to be able to climb trees like you do, Bree. You make it look so easy and so fun."

"Really?"

"Really."

"Tell you what…," I said slowly, trying to think of something that would make him feel better about the no-bathing thing. And then it hit me. "When this silly protest is over and the bylaw has been overturned, I'll teach you to climb safely."

"Really?"

"Really. Do you think your mom will let you?" I asked.

"If the bylaw is overturned, I think she could be convinced."

"Okay, so we have a deal?"

"Deal," Ethan said, looking happier than I'd seen him in a long time.

Making Ethan happy made me feel good for the rest of the day. But really, I didn't know when or if it would ever be possible for me to teach Ethan to climb. Even if the bylaw was overturned, I had my doubts about Ethan being able to convince his mom to let him climb again.

It didn't help that the protest just sort of fizzled out after that. No one actually talked about ending the protest, but there were more clean faces around Cedar Grove every day.

By the end of the week, the only holdout was Tyler. But I was sure it wouldn't be long before his smell disgusted even him.

I lasted until Friday, when I was invited to Sarah's for a sleepover. If it had been just me and Sarah, I might have held out longer. But she invited two other girls from her basketball team. I didn't know them very well, and I didn't want to feel self-conscious. Plus I was worried they might judge me before I had a chance to explain about the tree-climbing protest.

Man, did it feel good to be clean. And I had fun at the sleepover.

Did I mention how good it was to be clean? Even though I felt really bad about giving up on the protest, I knew there wasn't much point to it anymore. The Cedar Grove Neighborhood Council was never going to listen to us. Bath or no bath, it made no difference. Nothing did.

Chapter 13

The Friday night sleepover at Sarah's was the kickoff to the Easter long weekend, which was a big deal in Cedar Grove. A bunch of the moms, not including mine, always organized a big community Easter egg hunt. They were really serious about it. They even printed up a map of Cedar Grove so we would know where to look.

Despite the rain, everyone came out for the egg hunt. The Cedar Grove moms had put in a ton of work, and the younger kids were superexcited. I wondered if maybe I had outgrown this kind of silly fun. But all the kids were into it, even Tyler. And there was chocolate involved.

The idea behind the map was simple. Cedar Grove had been divided into three different zones. In the first zone, the area closest to the townhouses, the eggs were really easy to find. I mean *really easy*; I think I spotted at least ten as I walked from my front door to the courtyard. But I didn't touch any of them. That area was meant for the really little kids, like Sammy.

In the second zone, the eggs were a little harder to find, but still pretty easy. That area was for the kids Ethan's age. Most of the eggs were hidden in zone two because the majority of the kids in Cedar Grove were that age.

Zone three was my zone. It was the one farthest from the townhouses in an area bounded by the road, the river, and the railway tracks. The eggs were really hard to find in zone three. Even I found it challenging. And, of course, I was competing against kids like Michael and Tyler (but mostly Tyler).

As soon as Mrs. Williams shouted, "Let the hunt begin," I sprinted as fast as I could to the edge of our property. I had a copy of the map stuffed in my back pocket even though I was certain I knew everything there was to know about Cedar Grove. I just didn't want to risk getting caught collecting eggs in zone two. That would be bad.

I headed toward the river and the railway tracks. I figured that's where most of the eggs would be hidden since the moms didn't want us going too close to the road. And there weren't many hiding spots in the field between Cedar Grove and the other town-house complex.

Within minutes I had found two eggs. One under a rock and one hidden by the branch of a thorny bush. No way was I too old for an Easter egg hunt! This was fun!

I continued to search along the pathway that served as the border between Cedar Grove and the Fraser River. I looked around the lampposts, on the benches and even in the garbage bins.

Of course, I was hoping to avoid Tyler. And, of course, he showed up when I was looking through the garbage. As I lifted my head from the bin, there he was.

"Need something new to wear for Easter dinner?" Tyler smirked.

"Actually, I was just looking for you. I thought you might be in there," I said, pointing to the garbage can.

Tyler was too cool to carry an Easter basket. He was carrying a pillowcase instead. And I could see there were already a couple of eggs inside. "How's the egg hunt going?" he said.

"It was great fun until you came along," I replied.

"Well, don't get distracted and start climbing trees." Tyler winked. "Being the honest guy that I am, I'd have to report you to the Neighborhood Council."

"You like that bylaw, don't you?" I accused.

"I'm not the one who gave up on our protest."

"I haven't given up," I snapped.

"It sure smells like you have." For a minute I thought he was saying that I smelled like garbage. Then I realized he was talking about the fact that I'd had a bath. I was about to be on the other end of the conversation I'd had with Ethan and Ashley.

"Yeah, well"—I hesitated—"the no-bathing thing wasn't working. It was a stupid idea."

"It wasn't a stupid idea. It wasn't working because you people don't have enough backbone to follow through."

"What happened to your backbone when Ms. Matheson came out?"

"I'm wasting my time talking to you," Tyler said. "I've got eggs to find."

He turned and walked away. Toward the river.

I turned toward the railway tracks to get away from Tyler and his stink. Just beyond the tracks I spotted three trees that looked perfect for hiding eggs. I searched all the low branches but found nothing. I was surprised the Cedar Grove moms, who had so much experience with this Easter Bunny stuff, would miss such a great egg-hiding opportunity.

Curious, I checked the map. Surprised, I looked again.

There was no doubt about it. These trees were outside the Cedar Grove property line. Just over the border.

This was huge! I'd found trees—great trees—I could climb! Legally! Near my house! I wanted desperately to climb those trees right then and there. But I knew I shouldn't, and I didn't. Tyler was still lurking around, and I was expected back from the egg hunt soon.

I told myself to proceed with caution. If only I had listened.

Chapter 14

I waited three whole days to return for my first climb. Not because I wanted to. Because it took that long for the rain to stop.

The bark felt damp as I grabbed the highest branch I could reach and swung my feet upward. From there, I slowly made my way up into the tree, one branch at a time, staying close to the trunk. When the branches started to crowd in on me, I climbed out. There were only a couple of branches at that height that were thick enough to support my weight. I was high. About five feet from the top. I looked around. I could see the river, the train tracks and the east side of Cedar Grove. But I was pretty sure no one in Cedar Grove could see me. The trees were too far away from the townhouse.

And I was wearing my camouflage capri pants and a green shirt just to be safe.

Sarah sat below me, pretending to be on the lookout. She'd lost interest in climbing a long time ago. She was the sportiest girl I knew, but she wasn't the best tree climber in the world.

Of the three trees, the one closest to the tracks was easiest to climb. I thought of it as the Spoon. It's big, thick trunk was covered in smooth bark. Several large branches fanned out from the tree at waist height. All the branches were widely spaced and sloped up at a gentle angle giving the top of the tree a nice round shape. Sarah had already been up and down the Spoon twice.

The Fork, the tree I was in, was tougher. Its branches started higher up the trunk and then jutted out at a ninety-degree angle. A few feet away from the trunk, each branch took a sudden turn so that it looked like the tine of a fork. The flat surfaces of the tree made it easy to move around. But the angles were tricky, especially where the branches went straight up.

I hadn't yet tackled the third tree, the Knife, but I knew it was going to be a challenge. Every one of its branches went straight up with very little slope or angle. There were no flat surfaces at all.

I also knew, because Sarah was now sitting upright instead of lounging around, that there wasn't going to be time for anymore climbing today.

"Can we do something else now, Bree?" Sarah called up to me.

"Like what?" I asked.

"Let's go see what everyone else is doing."

"Like who?"

"Come on, Bree, let's just go."

"All right," I said. But I took my time getting down.

"You're sure those trees aren't on Cedar Grove property?" Sarah asked as we walked toward the townhouse complex. "It's pretty hard to see where the property line is."

"It's really clear on the map I got at the Easter egg hunt," I told her, "but I'm not sure how accurate the map is."

"Well, it probably doesn't matter," Sarah said as she ripped the foil off a chocolate Easter egg she had retrieved from her pocket. "You can still use the map to defend yourself if you get caught. I don't think you should worry about that silly bylaw anyway."

"But Tyler will turn me over to the Neighborhood Council if he sees me in a tree. Any tree. And I don't want to face them again. That would be bad." I shuddered, thinking about it.

"Tyler's not out to get you," Sarah said. "He's just competitive. And he likes to tease you because he always gets such a big reaction."

"Tease? He's mean, Sarah. Maybe you don't get it because he's nicer when you're around."

Sarah shrugged and handed me a chocolate.

I didn't say anything as I took the egg. I was mad at her for defending Tyler. Maybe I was right about them liking each other. Yuck.

As we got closer to Cedar Grove, I could hear the skippers chanting, *Ice-cream sundae, banana split*..." For once I wanted to join them, just to avoid Tyler.

But Sarah was heading straight toward the garage with the basketball hoop. Tyler's garage. I listened, hoping to hear a street hockey game over the skipping song, but there was only the sound of a ball bouncing against the pavement.

"Hey, Tyler," Sarah called out as we got close.

"Sarah. Bree. Wanna play?" Tyler took a shot and missed the net.

"Air ball," I said under my breath.

"I'll play," Sarah said, giving me a dirty look. Sarah's a good basketball player. I mean *really* good. We don't usually play together because she beats me every time. I had no doubt she'd give Tyler a close game.

"Where's Michael?" I asked.

"Dentist," Tyler replied as he passed the ball to Sarah.

"You two play one-on-one," I said. "I'll sit out." I didn't know exactly what was going on with Tyler and Sarah. Whatever it was, I didn't like it and I didn't want to be a part of it. I just wanted to do some more climbing.

I sat down on Ethan's front step and watched. Sarah was already up three to one.

Within minutes, Ethan was sitting next to me.

I was glad to see him. Glad to have someone to distract me from the basketball match. "What've you been doing?" I asked.

"Reading. Just finished my book."

"Why don't you play video games or something?" I asked, although it wasn't really a question. And because I was feeling miserable, I added, "You know, like other kids."

Ethan just shrugged. "I like to read."

"Where's your mom?"

"Getting ready for some big meeting," Ethan replied.

"A Cedar Grove Neighborhood Council meeting?"

"Nah. Something at the school."

Poor Ethan. His mom would never let him spend time playing video games. And she was never around to do anything fun with him. Good thing he had me and the rest of the Cedar Grove kids.

"Want to play catch?" Ethan asked. "Help me test my arm a bit?"

"Sorry, Ethan," I said, feeling bad about disappointing him. "I have to walk Sarah home as soon as she's done this game. Then it'll be time for dinner."

We sat in silence for a few minutes, watching the basketball game. Sarah was up seven to six. Tyler was still smiling and joking around even though she was winning. Why was I the only one he hated losing to?

I tried to think of something funny to share with Ethan. Something to change the mood. And that's when I remembered my promise.

"Listen," I said as quietly as I could, "were you serious about learning to climb trees?"

Ethan looked at me, his forehead wrinkled with confusion.

"Yeah, I guess," he said slowly.

"Then let's do it," I said, keeping my voice down.

"But how? It's illegal."

"I found some trees. They're not on Cedar Grove property." I was whispering now.

"I'm not allowed to leave Cedar Grove without my mom's permission," Ethan said miserably.

"But they are ALMOST on the property."

"You know how my mom is about rules, Bree."

"I know, I know. Just come with me tomorrow after school. You can stay on Cedar Grove property and watch me climb. I'll teach you what I can, and if you get bored, we'll play catch."

"Really?" Ethan said, his voice rising with excitement. "And there will be no risk of a fine?"

"Shhhhh." I smiled and made a slight movement of my head in Tyler's direction. "It's all legal, but I don't want everyone finding out about the trees." I really didn't need any more trouble from Tyler. And if the Easter egg map was wrong, I didn't want to know. That would be bad.

"Should I wear camouflage?" Ethan said, gesturing toward my capris.

"You don't need camouflage. You won't be that close to the trees. Just meet me by the mailboxes tomorrow at four. And bring your glove."

"Okay, but I doubt I'll need my glove. I won't get bored watching you climb. I think I'll bring my notebook instead so I can write down all the things I learn!"

"Bring whatever you want, Ethan, but remember, this is supposed to be fun." I was suddenly having doubts. How much could Ethan learn if he couldn't go into the trees? And what if his mom didn't even want him watching? Was there some way she could stop me from climbing those trees too?

But Ethan was excited. And the basketball game was over. It was too late now.

Sarah had won. She gave Tyler a high five that lasted longer than it needed to and then turned to me. "Let's go, Bree. I gotta get home before Dad kills me."

"See you tomorrow. But remember, the trees are a secret," I whispered to Ethan as I stood up to leave.

He looked up and nodded, all smiles.

Chapter 15

Teaching Ethan to climb was fun. For a few days he only watched, just as we'd planned, but soon he couldn't stop himself from getting into the Spoon. I tried to convince him to follow his mom's rule and stay on Cedar Grove property, but the trees were so close and, well, Ethan was desperate to do some climbing himself. I couldn't really blame him and there was nothing I could do to stop him.

After a couple of days on the Spoon, he was ready to try the Fork. I could get to the top of it by then, but I had to plan my route carefully. I gave Ethan a few pointers and let him attempt the Fork alone. I think he scraped his knees a couple of times but he never fell.

When he got tired, he'd sit on the other side of the Cedar Grove property line and watch me tackle the Knife. I was getting closer to the top every day. But I didn't push too hard. It was fun watching Ethan learn, and I knew that once I had the Knife figured out, I'd be desperate to find new trees to climb. And that would be bad, since there weren't any.

"You're such a good climber," Ethan said to me when I plopped down next to him on the grass one day. We'd been climbing together for a week. I wasn't sure I had anything more to teach Ethan. The rest was just practice.

"So are you. Helps that you have a great teacher!" I said, laughing.

Ethan smiled.

"You've really practiced hard," I said. "Doesn't your Mom wonder what you've been up to these last few days?"

"I guess she'll expect me to be pretty good at baseball," Ethan said, looking at the gloves that lay on the grass beside us, unused. "But she's too busy to care. And she's not worried as long as I'm with you."

"Really?"

"Yup, she thinks you're very responsible. She talked about it after you gave that presentation to the Neighborhood Council."

"Really?" I said again. I was surprised. Especially since the council hadn't listened to anything I had said. And Ms. Matheson's words, *You do not set the best example, Brianna*, had stuck with me.

"Yup."

"Well, that's good," I said as I lay back on the grass, letting the sun hit my face.

"Um, I have a favor to ask, Bree," Ethan said.

"What?"

"Well, it's just that some of the other Cedar Grove kids would like to learn how to climb too."

"Like who?" I asked, not really paying attention to what he was saying. I was enjoying the warmth and the fact that someone thought I was responsible. I was proud that Ms. Matheson had been impressed by my presentation to the council, even if it had been a waste of time.

"Like Salina."

I bolted upward, momentarily blinded by the sun. "How does Salina know I'm teaching you to climb?"

"Oh, I might have told her," Ethan said as if it were no big deal.

"Ethan! The trees were supposed to be a secret!" I could feel the blood rushing to my cheeks. I'm sure my face turned a thousand shades of red.

Ethan looked at me anxiously. "But Salina promised she wouldn't tell. And I didn't tell anyone else."

"A secret is NOT something you tell one person at a time," I stammered.

"It's just that I was so excited about it and I wanted to tell someone, and now Salina is excited too and so I was just wondering if you could teach her to climb." Ethan looked as if he was about to cry.

I lay back down, hitting my head hard against the ground. What was I going to do now? If I started teaching other kids how to climb, it was only a matter of time before everyone, including the Cedar Grove Neighborhood Council, found out. I wasn't even sure it was legal to be climbing these trees. I was probably breaking another bylaw. And even if it was legal, the other parents might still think I was putting their kids in danger. I was sure the council would kick us out of our house for that.

On the other hand, if I refused to teach Salina to climb, she might get mad and tell people anyway. And knowing about the rivalry between Tyler and me, she would definitely go to him first.

I couldn't believe I'd gotten myself into this. All I'd done is offered to let Ethan watch me climb. The rest had just happened.

After I had calmed down and thought it through, I finally said, "Okay, Ethan. Bring her tomorrow."

"Thanks, Bree. Really, thanks. That's great."

Ethan looked so relieved that I almost smiled. But instead I glared at him with my best principal face and said, "But you must promise not to tell anyone else."

"Not a word." Ethan clamped his lips together between two fingers and gave me the thumbs-up with the other hand.

If only I believed him.

Chapter 16

"Okay, that's good. Now reach up with your left hand. No, left. The other hand. You can do it. Keep your foot on the branch until you've grabbed hold of the…"

"Bree?" Salina said urgently.

"What is it, Salina?"

"I think I need a break."

"Okay." I sighed. "Come on down. Do you need help?"

"No. I can do it. Just give me a minute," she called down.

She wasn't even that high. I rolled my eyes. Teaching Salina was much tougher than teaching Ethan.

I turned and walked over to the grass where a group of kids was sitting next to the railway tracks. "Who's next?" I asked.

"My turn!" Ashley jumped up, blond hair bouncing.

Sure enough, my tree-climbing lessons were a "secret" that was spreading through Cedar Grove, one kid at a time. It seemed that suddenly everyone was interested in learning how to climb trees. Maybe because it was illegal without really being illegal. Or something like that. But some kids were definitely better than others. Ashley was surprisingly good. She wore pink even when she climbed (in shorts not skirts), but she was actually kind of fun to be around when she wasn't skipping.

We walked over to the Spoon and waited for Salina to come down. Only one kid was allowed on the Spoon at a time. And they had to be supervised, by me, at all times. I wasn't taking any chances on someone getting hurt. That would be bad.

I looked up at Ethan. He was in the Fork. When I decided someone was good enough for the Fork, I allowed them to climb it on their own. I was still around, just not watching their every move.

And they had to follow the rules I'd come up with to keep everyone safe.

Safety was my number-one concern. If anyone got hurt, the secret would get out for sure. And I had no doubt that big trouble would follow.

I wondered why more parents weren't suspicious of the scrapes covering everyone's elbows and knees. Maybe they just figured it was a natural part of the weather warming up and skin being exposed. But really, these kids must be going through a lot of Band-Aids.

Ethan smiled and waved. He really loved tree climbing. Almost as much as me.

"Okay, Ashley. Your turn," I said when Salina finally emerged at the bottom of the Spoon.

As Ashley stepped onto the lower branch, I heard a deep voice behind me yell, "What's going on here?"

I turned around, heart pounding. It was Tyler. Michael was standing behind him.

"What are you doing here, Tyler?" I said quickly, trying to act calmer than I felt.

"No, the question is"—Tyler looked around at all the kids—"what are YOU all doing here?"

"Climbing trees," I said, looking him right in the eye. There was no way to hide it. I couldn't believe we'd managed to keep it from him for this long. And I knew right away that was the part that was really going to make him angry. I wished Sarah was here to give him a reason to be nicer to me.

"As I'm sure you all know," Tyler said, "that is against Cedar Grove bylaws."

"No, it's not," Ethan said. "These trees are not on Cedar Grove property."

I turned and stared at Ethan. I was surprised he wasn't hiding up in the tree. Even more surprised at the conviction in his voice. It didn't sound like him at all.

"Tell him, Bree," Ethan said.

"Ethan's right, Tyler. These trees are not on Cedar Grove property."

"How do you know?" Michael asked.

"I've got a map that proves it," I said.

"This sure looks like Cedar Grove property to me," Tyler said. "And I think the Neighborhood Council would be very interested to know that you've been climbing these trees."

"You're not going to tell them!" Salina gasped. "We could get fined! Our families could get kicked out of Cedar Grove!"

"The Neighborhood Council needs to know. And they need to know that not only has Bree been climbing trees"—Tyler paused for effect—"she's also been encouraging all of you to do it too."

"We're here because we want to be here," Ethan said, still sounding unusually forceful. "It's not Bree's fault."

Everyone was silent.

"How 'bout we settle this with a tree-climbing contest?" Michael suggested, breaking the silence.

"A tree-climbing contest?" I asked.

"Yeah. A climbing competition. Between you and Tyler."

"Good idea!" Ethan said. "Whoever gets highest in the Knife wins the competition."

"Or we could see who can get to the top of that tree the fastest." Michael was pointing at the Fork.

"No contest," said Salina. "Bree would win for sure."

"Win what?" Tyler asked.

"Your silence," said Ethan.

"Yeah. If Bree wins, Tyler has to promise not to say anything. If Tyler wins, Bree has to go back to the council and confess." As Michael said this, I noticed

Tyler's eyes dart toward him. Tyler looked angry. And maybe a little scared.

One of the kids started chanting, "*Bree! Bree! Bree! Bree!*" Soon other voices joined in. My body started tingling with anticipation. Every muscle in my body tensed, ready for the climb.

But there was also a nagging voice in my head, telling me that this wasn't a good idea. Even though I knew I could beat Tyler, competitive tree climbing wasn't safe. Not without ropes and harnesses and all that stuff that was on the TCI website. This seemed like a sure way for someone to get hurt. Most likely it would be Tyler. And even I didn't want that. I just wanted him to stop competing with me.

"*Bree! Bree! Bree!*" The kids were still chanting, but they were starting to lose their enthusiasm since neither me or Tyler were saying a word.

Then Sammy started to cry, and all the chanting stopped.

"I think he's been stung by a bee," Salina announced.

"Take him home," I said to her. "You should all go home," I added, hoping that Tyler would be easier to deal with if he didn't have an audience to impress.

Tyler and I stared at each other, arms crossed, while we waited for everyone to leave. Ethan wanted to stay, but I told him to go. "Make sure none of the other kids tell their parents about the trees," I whispered to him as he walked away. "This isn't over yet."

And then everyone was gone, except for Michael, who was standing behind Tyler and looking up into the trees. Tyler and I kept staring at each other, neither of us wanting to be the first to speak.

"It would be great!" Michael finally said. "I could charge admission. Sell popcorn. Make it into a real community event!"

"Community event?" I said. "Yeah, right. And you think you could do all that without the Neighborhood Council and the rest of the parents finding out?"

"She's right," Tyler said, turning his glare on Michael. "Besides, I have nothing to gain from a climb-off."

"Afraid you'll lose?" I couldn't resist.

"No," Tyler said flatly.

"But if you win, Bree has to confess!" Michael said.

"What do I care if she confesses?" Tyler snapped.

"You expect me to believe that you don't want me to get in trouble? You really are afraid to lose!"

I felt better now that I knew Tyler didn't want to compete. But there was still a part of me that really wanted to beat him.

"I'm not afraid to lose. But like I said, I have nothing to gain from a climb-off. There's not gonna be a tree-climbing contest," Tyler said firmly.

"So then," I said slowly, "what's it going to take to keep you quiet?"

Tyler looked around to make sure Michael wasn't listening. "Maybe there is something you could do for me," he said.

"What?" I asked.

"Can you give Sarah a message for me?"

"What?" I couldn't believe what I was hearing.

"A message. For Sarah," Tyler repeated, clearly embarrassed.

"If I give Sarah a message, will you promise to keep your mouth shut about the tree climbing?" I said this slowly, enjoying Tyler's discomfort.

Tyler nodded.

"Aren't you worried about what the other kids will think? That you backed away from a tree-climbing contest?"

"No. The kids around here look up to me. And like I've already said a million times, I have nothing to gain from winning a tree-climbing competition. Will you give Sarah a message if I promise not to go to the council?"

This boy-girl stuff was a mystery to me. "Why don't you just give Sarah a ring? I mean, phone call?" I said, catching myself. I was getting flustered and starting to talk like an English schoolgirl again.

"Listen, Bree," Tyler said impatiently, "do we have a deal or not?"

"Deal," I said quickly before he changed his mind. "What's the message?"

"I'll write it down," he mumbled, "and drop it in your mailbox."

"Okay."

"Let's go, Michael." Tyler had already turned to leave.

Michael smiled at me before trotting off after Tyler. "Too bad about the tree-climbing competition."

"Yeah, too bad." I smiled back.

Chapter 17

Sure enough, the note was in my mailbox when I left for school the next morning. I read it, of course. I figured there was no way Tyler would know I had read it and I was sure that Sarah wouldn't mind. Pretty sure anyway.

All it said was, *REMATCH*. It was written in perfect block letters. Almost as if Tyler had written it over and over again until he got it just right. He'd used red ink.

I could've told Sarah about the note when we met by the swings before school started. But for some reason, I waited until lunch.

Before handing her the note, I described the show-down between Tyler and me. Sarah didn't say much. She just nodded patiently and then slowly unfolded the note. She took way too long to read it—it was only one word after all—and then she folded it back up again. She set it on the edge of her lunch tray and continued eating.

"So?" I said.

"So what?" she said as she peeled her banana.

"Don't you think it's weird? That he'd pass on an opportunity to get me into heaps of trouble?"

"Not really. Tyler's not as bad as you think."

I sighed. I couldn't remember anything that Sarah and I had ever disagreed on. Until now. "So you're going to give him a rematch? I'm assuming he means basketball?"

"Maybe. We'll see." Sarah was diving into her bag of cookies now. She seemed totally disinterested.

"But if you don't give him a rematch, he'll think I didn't give you the note and then he'll go blabbing to the Neighborhood Council."

"Relax, Bree. Tyler's not going to tell. Besides, they're bound to find out sooner or later. There's no way a big group of kids can keep a secret like that."

I didn't say anything. I knew she was right, but I was mad at her for saying it. We both ate quietly until the bell rang.

"Are you coming over after school?" I asked before she left.

"Not tonight," she said. I watched as she dumped what was left on her lunch tray into the garbage. But not before she pocketed the note from Tyler.

I was miserable for the rest of the day. I kept thinking about what Sarah had said. I might be safe from Tyler, but no matter what either of us did, the council was bound to find out about the tree climbing eventually.

When I got home from school, Ethan was waiting in the usual spot next to the mailboxes. There were three other kids with him, all holding baseball gloves. I made a mental note to bring bats next time. Parents must be getting suspicious about all this catching practice.

"So?" Ethan said anxiously.

"Tyler's not going to tell."

"What happened? Did you do a climb-off? I can't believe I missed it! I would have loved to see you beat him!" Ethan rambled on, clearly relieved.

"I don't really want to talk about it, Ethan," I said. "And I think we should take a couple days off from climbing. Until things cool down, you know?"

Ethan nodded miserably. "Sure, Bree. Want to play catch instead?"

"Not now. Sorry, Ethan." I smiled at him. "I've got a lot on my mind."

"Okay."

"I'll see you later." I walked around the corner and grabbed my bike from the garage. I cycled along the Fraser River until I was sure no one was watching. Then I turned and headed toward the railway tracks. To my trees.

I hid my bike behind a bush and started climbing up into the Knife. I cleared my mind and concentrated on the branch in front of me. Within ten minutes I was as high as I could safely go. I wasn't going to reach the top today.

I sat on a branch near the trunk and let my feet swing freely below me. It felt good to be surrounded by big green leaves. I heard a bee buzz by my ear, lured by the sweet smell of tree sap. It was one of those cloudy Vancouver days where the gray sky seemed close enough to reach up and touch. The clouds were like a blanket that warmed the air without any help from the sun. I felt like I could hide away on this branch forever.

And then, suddenly, I saw a branch move in the tree next to me. Actually, the whole tree started moving. And I could hear the sound of twigs breaking. There was something in the Fork.

I sat there as quietly as I could. Whatever it was, it was too large to be a squirrel or a cat. It sounded like a person, but I was sure Ethan would've told the Cedar Grove kids to stay away. I watched and waited for something—or someone—to appear.

Within minutes I saw a hand reach up to a thick branch parallel to the one I was sitting on. Then I heard a grunt as a knee appeared next to the hand. Another hand. Another knee.

It was Michael.

"Hi," I said quietly, not wanting to scare him. I was pretty sure he didn't know I was there.

"Oh!" Michael turned quickly and almost lost his balance. "Hi," he said once he was steady again.

"I didn't know you liked to climb trees," I said.

"Neither did I. I'm not very good at it. But when I saw you all crowded around these trees yesterday, I decided I had to give it another shot." Michael smiled at me. "It's fun!"

"Does Tyler know you're here?"

"Nope."

"I've never seen you go anywhere without him."

"Come on, Bree, I'm not that bad. He's not that bad. He just likes to give you a hard time because you're so good at sports." Michael paused, then quietly added, "Plus, you're a natural leader. Tyler isn't. His baseball coach is always on his case about it. He watches you do all this stuff—teaching kids to climb, organizing protests—and it makes him crazy."

I looked at Michael, trying to figure out if he was making fun of me. He appeared to be serious. "Sarah's good at sports too," I said.

"That's different."

I didn't understand. And I didn't want to talk about Tyler and Sarah. So instead I asked, "Do you really think Tyler will keep quiet about the tree climbing?"

"Yeah. He really likes Sarah. He doesn't want to do anything to get her mad at him."

"Oh." So I was right. But I still had no idea whether Sarah liked him back. And she was supposed to be my best friend.

"But, Bree?"

"Yeah?"

"Don't you think it would be better if the tree climbing wasn't a secret?" Michael was looking quite comfortable now, perched in the tree with his back against the trunk.

"What do you mean?" I asked.

"You should keep up your fight against the bylaw. Then we could climb at Cedar Grove again. Without worrying about getting caught."

"But the Neighborhood Council didn't listen to me. And they ignored our protest. What else can I do?"

"According to my dad, safety is the issue," Michael said.

I rolled my eyes. *Safety, safety, safety*—I was so tired of that word!

Michael continued, "And Ethan says you've come up with all kinds of rules to keep kids safe while you are teaching them to climb."

I rolled my eyes again. Ethan just couldn't keep his mouth shut!

"So maybe if you explained how you've made tree climbing safe for everyone in Cedar Grove, the council would reconsider."

"But I can't do another presentation," I blurted out. "I don't even think they'll let me."

"What about the Annual General Meeting?"

"What about it?"

"The AGM is scheduled for the end of the month. It's an open meeting for every resident in Cedar Grove."

"You want me to give a presentation in front of everyone in Cedar Grove?"

"Well," Michael said, "my dad says the tree-climbing bylaw won't be official until there's another vote."

"That's just some kind of formality. The council has already made their decision."

"But my dad is a council member and he doesn't agree with the bylaw."

"He doesn't?" I couldn't keep the surprise out of my voice.

"No. And he says he'll vote against it at the upcoming AGM."

"You mean there is actually going to be a vote?"

"Of course." Michael gave me a funny look. "Right now it's just something called an interim bylaw.

It won't be a *real* bylaw unless it passes the vote at the AGM."

"Really?" What Michael was saying sounded familiar, but it was taking my brain a while to catch up. "Are you sure?"

"Yes," Michael said. "And the way I see it, if you can convince the residents of Cedar Grove—not just the Council—that tree climbing is safe, you can stop the bylaw from becoming a real and permanent thing."

I started nodding. Slowly. Then I smiled. Michael was smarter than I'd ever given him credit for.

"It's worth a try," I said quietly.

"If anyone can do it, you can, Bree."

I swallowed hard. Another presentation. A much bigger presentation in front of everyone, not just the Neighborhood Council.

The idea made me nervous, but for some reason, I didn't feel scared. Not like last time. Michael's confidence made me feel hopeful.

Maybe a little too hopeful.

Chapter 18

I stood at the front of the common room. Ethan stood beside me. My heart was beating fast, but it wasn't thumping wildly like it had the last time I was in this room. I was more confident about what I had to say this time, but there was a lot at stake.

The council members were seated at the long conference table beside us. They had just called for a short break to discuss some picky detail in the Neighborhood Act. Apparently, they needed to sort it out before the meeting could proceed. The AGM had started at 6:30 PM. It was already 8:00 PM. "Let's just get on with it!" I wanted to yell. Waiting was hard.

In front of the Neighborhood Council sat rows and rows of Cedar Grove residents. I looked around.

There was grouchy old Mrs. Leary, front and center. She had three different sweaters wrapped around her, despite the heat, and she looked like she was about to fall asleep. Mom and Dad were sitting directly behind her. I could tell they were holding hands, as usual. In the next row, Ashley sat next to her dad. Beside them, Sammy and Salina were squashed between both parents, who were desperately trying to keep Sammy still.

Toward the back I saw Michael. He was looking at me, so I smiled. He smiled back and gave me a thumbs-up. It made me feel good. Maybe just because of the confidence he had in me. Or maybe it was something more.

Sitting next to Michael was Tyler. I was surprised to see him. He knew that Sarah wasn't going to be at the meeting. He'd asked me about it yesterday. He'd also wished me luck with my presentation. Did he care about the bylaw after all? Or was it possible that, instead of resenting me, he was starting to respect me, like Michael seemed to think?

There were a lot more Cedar Grove kids there than I expected. Especially considering we weren't allowed to vote. I guess I wasn't the only one who felt there was a lot at stake.

Finally, Ms. Matheson cleared her throat and said, "The next item on our agenda is the ratification of bylaw 47.21. Please have the minutes reflect that Brianna Bridges, Unit 83, and Ethan Matheson, Unit 49, have asked to address the residents of Cedar Grove prior to the vote."

Ms. Matheson paused and waited for the room to settle. When everything was quiet and still, she said, "Go ahead, Brianna," looking directly at me and ignoring the fact that her son was standing proudly at my side.

"Thank you, Ms. Matheson," I said as confidently as I could. "And I'd like to thank the Neighborhood Council for providing us with this opportunity. Ethan and I have put together a PowerPoint presentation to illustrate why we think tree climbing is a fun and safe activity that should be allowed in Cedar Grove."

I turned to Ethan. He took the cue, not looking at all nervous. "Bree has been teaching me to climb trees outside Cedar Grove property."

Ms. Matheson scowled and narrowed her eyes. Mom frowned even though she already knew all about this. I'd told both Mom and Dad the whole story right after Michael convinced me to speak at the AGM. As usual, Dad was very supportive, and Mom—well, Mom was Mom.

Ethan went on. "I can climb quite high now and I have not fallen once. I have a few scrapes and bruises but nothing worse than I'd get from a game of street hockey. The important thing is, I love it. Tree climbing is fun. It makes me feel happy and free, and it helps me forget my problems." He looked at his mom when he said this.

"Bree's been teaching lots of us to climb," Ethan continued. "She's very good. And she makes sure everyone stays at a level where they are safe. No one can move higher until she decides they are ready."

Without hesitation, Ethan proceeded through the PowerPoint presentation that Dad had helped him prepare. His voice was loud and clear, and he didn't make a single mistake.

When he was done, he turned toward me.

I took a deep breath and launched right into my part of the presentation.

"As Ethan has pointed out, tree climbing is very safe as long as it is done carefully under the right rules and guidelines." I flipped to my first slide. "Here is a list of rules that we have been following."

BREE'S RULES FOR
TREE-CLIMBING SAFETY

1. *Only climb using branches thicker than your wrist.*
2. *Keep two on the tree at all times (two hands, or two feet, or one hand and one foot).*
3. *Always have an exit plan that doesn't involve landing on your head. In other words, NEVER FORGET THE FALL!*

I read each rule aloud and offered to answer any questions anyone had about any of them. No one said anything, so I carried on.

"Here are some examples of how other groups have made tree climbing safe." I had a couple of slides that covered this topic. One was about a school that got a professional arborist or tree trimmer (I had to look that up) to do a hazard inspection once a year to ensure the trees in the area were safe to climb. Another set up a certification program where students had to go through a safety workshop and climbing instruction before they were allowed near the trees.

"Even without these types of precautions, backyard tree climbing is considered safer than most other recreational sports." I flipped to another slide.

The Top Ten Most Dangerous Sports for Kids

1. Basketball

2. Bicycling

3. Football

4. Soccer

5. Baseball

6. Skateboarding

7. Trampoline

8. Softball

9. Swimming and Diving

10. Horseback Riding

I went on to list other sports that lead to emergency-room visits, including weightlifting, volleyball, golf, roller-skating, wrestling, gymnastics, inline skating, tennis and track-and-field. And then I talked about cheerleading since it was listed in several places, including an official medical website, as the most dangerous female sport there was. Learning that had prompted me to search for something about skipping. To my surprise, I'd found out that skipping was a highly competitive sport. And that many elite athletes used it for cross-training because it was so safe. Was it possible that skipping with the Cedar Grove Girly-Girls could make me a better climber? Maybe I'd judged it all a little too harshly.

My last slide showed the map of Cedar Grove and the location of the Spoon, Fork and Knife. Dad had helped with this one by scanning the map of the Easter egg hunt into the computer.

"In conclusion, I'd just like to say that *people*—both kids and adults—have been climbing trees for… forever." I hadn't planned this part of the presentation but I felt the need to finish with something big. "It's fun, it's healthy, it's almost spiritual, and it can be very safe if it is done properly. You can't protect kids from everything. You can get hurt crossing the road. Banning tree climbing in Cedar Grove will not make us safer. It will just make us miserable."

There was some clapping at the back of the room. One of the Cedar Grove Girly-Girls yelled,

"No more bylaws!" Some of them had really taken my warning about skipping bylaws seriously. I felt kinda bad about that.

I still had everyone's attention. But I had nothing left to say. I allowed myself a deep sigh of relief.

The hard part was over. Or so I thought.

Chapter 19

"I will now open the floor for questions and comments prior to the vote." Ms. Matheson said the word *vote* the way Sarah said *math test*. Like there should be sinister music playing in the background. *Dun, dun, dun...*

My mouth was dry. I was thirsty from my presentation and suddenly very nervous about the vote. I looked over at Ethan, wondering if we should sit down. He smiled and stayed where he was. So I did too.

A man near the back of the room cleared his throat. "How accurate is that map?"

My heart started doing its Energizer Bunny routine. Why did the very first question have to be one that I couldn't answer?

Mrs. Williams, Ashley's mom, came to my rescue. "I'll speak to that," she said as she reached into the bag next to her and pulled out a rolled-up piece of paper. She unfolded it on the table in front of her. "I took the liberty of digging up the official map of Cedar Grove." She held up the map even though it was too small for anyone beyond the front row to see. "Those trees you've been using for lessons…what do you call them, Bree?"

"The Spoon, the Fork, and the Knife?"

"Yes, those. They are definitely not on Cedar Grove property," Mrs. Williams said firmly.

"So there is no legal liability attached to the climbing of those trees?" Michael's dad smiled as he spoke. He was sitting up front with the other council members. On his name tag he'd drawn *Daniel Morrow* in block letters like something from a cartoon. Beside it, he'd written *Call me Dan*. No wonder he and my dad were such good friends.

"None," said Mrs. Williams. "At least, not for Cedar Grove."

I hadn't realized until that moment that I'd stopped breathing. I finally inhaled. But my relief did not last long.

Someone from the audience spoke up. "What's this about legal liability?"

Before anyone could reply, Ms. Ambrosia, Sammy and Salina's mom, said, "I don't care if there is a legal liability or not. I don't want my kids hanging around the railroad tracks."

"But there hasn't been a train on those tracks in years," Dad said, "maybe decades."

"Well, I think banning tree climbing in our own backyard just encourages our kids to go farther away and there is nothing safe about that," Ms. Ambrosia shot back.

"I agree," said Peter's mom. "It's safer if they're closer."

"But some of the trees in Cedar Grove are really high. Someone could get killed!" I couldn't see who was talking, but whoever it was sounded angry.

There was a murmur in the crowd and then everyone started talking at once.

"Okay, okay, everyone calm down." Ms. Matheson stood up and spoke as if she was addressing a school assembly. "I'd like to take this opportunity to outline the position of the Neighborhood Council."

The room was quiet. It was her turn to have everyone's attention.

"As most of you know, the interim bylaw, which prohibits tree climbing on Cedar Grove property, was passed by the council prior to the AGM for safety reasons." Ms. Matheson paused and looked down at the table as if collecting her thoughts. "At first it was simple. Council members were worried because a child had been hurt climbing trees."

"Hurt badly?" asked Peter's mom. "Who was it?"

"That's not important. He's okay now," Ms. Matheson said quickly.

I glanced at Ethan who was standing very still and very straight. It looked like it was his turn to stop breathing.

"After the interim bylaw was passed, some people expressed concern, and their concern forced me to look into the bylaw in further detail. I found out that there is significant legal liability involved."

"Meaning?" Peter's mom prompted.

"We could get sued if a child gets hurt climbing trees on Cedar Grove property." Ms. Matheson words hung in the air as I took this in.

"But why would anyone sue the Neighborhood Council?" Ethan asked.

"It's happened before." Ms. Matheson did not look in our direction as she spoke. "A child in the States fell when climbing a tree at the local playground. He was seriously injured. The parents successfully sued the city and received enough money to cover medical expenses, loss of future potential and other damages."

"That kind of stuff doesn't happen here," said one of the men in the crowd.

"If only that were true," another retorted.

Ms. Matheson took control again. "On behalf of the Neighborhood Council, I looked at lots of options to try and protect Cedar Grove from that type of legal liability. According to our lawyers, all the options, including some that have been outlined by Ethan and Brianna, are just too difficult and expensive to execute effectively."

"What about having climbers or their parents sign waivers?" Dad asked.

"We thought about that," Ms. Matheson replied without hesitation. "Believe me, we looked at everything. In the end, we decided that bylaw 47.21 was the only way to completely protect Cedar Grove from being legally liable for potential damages associated with tree climbing on our property."

"So the bylaw has nothing to do with keeping our kids safe?" Sammy and Salina's mom asked. "It's all about protecting Cedar Grove from a lawsuit?"

"It is about keeping our kids safe. That's the only way to avoid legal liability," Ms. Matheson responded firmly, as if that should be the end of the story. Case closed.

"Are all the council members in agreement on this?" asked Peter's mom.

"The majority of us voted in favor of the interim bylaw," Ms. Matheson said, "and now it is time for all the members of Cedar Grove to vote."

"Unless anyone else has something to say?" said Dan Morrow.

There was silence. Ms. Matheson sat down. I felt silly, still standing at the front of the room, but I didn't know what else to do.

"Okay," Dan spoke again, "the ballot will take place by a show of hands. Remember, only one owner per unit is eligible to vote."

"I think we need more time to think before we vote," Mom said. "Given this new...this new information."

"I agree," someone said.

"We need to vote now," Ms. Matheson responded. It was the first time I'd ever seen her look flustered. "The bylaw is only an interim measure. Once the AGM is over, it will no longer be valid."

"Can we abstain?" Mom asked.

Ms. Matheson looked at Dan.

"Yes," Dan said. "You can choose not to vote." He referred momentarily to his notes and then looked back at Ms. Matheson. "So, I guess we'll proceed?"

"Get on with it," Ms. Matheson growled.

Dan looked uncomfortable. Slowly he said, "All in favor of bylaw 47.21, please raise your hands."

There was a flurry of activity. I closed my eyes. When I opened them, I saw more hands in the air than I wanted to see.

There was silence as Michael's dad counted. I tried to count as well, but I kept losing track. I was too worked up to concentrate. The only thing I know for sure is that neither Mom's or Dad's hand was in the air.

"Okay." Dan was writing and talking slowly. "Now all opposed to bylaw 47.21, please raise your hands."

This time I didn't close my eyes. I watched as a bunch of arms shot up quickly, including Dad's. Slowly, more reluctant hands joined them in the air. I waited and watched. It didn't look like enough.

Actually, it looked like the same number of hands that had gone up in favor of the bylaw.

There was more silence and more counting. Dan scratched his head. He looked at his papers again. Then, with a puzzled look on his face, he said, "How many abstainers?"

To my surprise, several hands went up, including two belonging to council members. I looked to see if Mom had raised her hand, and then I realized that Dad had voted for both of them. I wondered how Mom felt about that. Her eyebrows weren't giving anything away.

"Interesting," I heard Ethan murmur quietly beside me.

It didn't take Dan long to count this time, but the puzzled look did not leave his face. He whispered something to the council member sitting next to him. Then he said, "The vote appears to be tied."

"What does that mean?" someone in the audience asked.

"Right now there are not enough votes to ratify the bylaw."

"But there are absentee ballots to consider!" Ms. Matheson blurted out. "And too many people are abstaining!" She looked at the other council members accusingly.

"Yes," Dan said thoughtfully, "I think we need to consider a secret ballot. This is clearly a contentious issue among residents." He paused, waiting for a reaction. There wasn't any. It was like everyone was in shock.

Finally, Ms. Matheson spoke up. "We need to continue with the AGM. There are other items on the agenda."

"To ensure an accurate result, I think it is best if we give everyone some time to think. I will collect the votes after the AGM," Dan said. "Unfortunately, that means the result will not be available until the end of the week."

The room suddenly felt stuffy. As if everyone had exhaled at once.

"Very well," said Ms. Matheson curtly. "We will now move to the next item on the agenda."

I turned to gather my things. I was ready to go. And apparently I wasn't the only one who didn't want to stay for the rest of the meeting. The sound of metal chair legs against linoleum floor filled the room as others stood to leave. The rest of the agenda was routine council stuff. There was nothing left to vote on.

We walked as a pack through our townhouse complex with a group of parents trailing behind. One by one, my friends peeled off to their own little piece of Cedar Grove and disappeared behind different doorways.

We reached Michael's townhouse too soon. I liked walking next to him. I felt grateful to him, for sure, but I knew it was more than that. I suddenly understood why Tyler was so different around Sarah. So nice.

We reached Tyler's driveway last. Before turning off the road, he punched me gently on the shoulder and said, "I couldn't have done that, Bree."

"You didn't have to."

"Yeah, but now I have to practice so I can beat you to the top of a tree."

"If the bylaw is overturned," I said with a nervous laugh.

"It will be."

We exchanged a smile, and then he was gone.

"You really knocked that one out of the park, Bree," Dad said as he swung an imaginary baseball bat through the air.

"Thanks," I said, "but we still don't know what's going to happen with the bylaw."

"Well," said Dad, "at least you ensured the vote was fair and informed."

Mom was silent as she unlocked our front door. Just as she was about to step inside she turned to me and said, "I'm proud of you, Brianna."

My mouth went dry and my chest warmed up as if I'd eaten something hot and spicy. Heat spread through me until my fingers and toes were tingling with happiness.

In some ways I was glad that it was going to take a while to hear from the Neighborhood Council again. I didn't want the good feeling to go away.

Chapter 20

Ding Dong.

"Brianna? Are you going to get the door?" Mom yelled out from across the hall.

"I'm reading!" I yelled back. "Just like you wanted me to!"

I was following Mom and Dad's advice not to climb the Spoon, Fork, or Knife until the council sorted out the bylaw. Their advice made sense. Although it was technically legal to climb those trees, I didn't want to upset anyone who might be considering a "no" vote. But I suspected Mom had another motive. She wanted me inside, working on my end-of-the-year school project. And I wanted to be outside, climbing trees!

Ding Dong. Somehow, the doorbell sounded more urgent the second time.

"Brianna!" And so did Mom. I could tell by her voice that her eyebrows were scrunched.

"What?"

"It's for you."

"Tell whoever it is that you've trapped me in my room so I can't come out and play."

"It's Ms. Matheson."

What was she doing here?

"Come down please, Brianna."

I sighed and put my bookmark in place. I was only on page two, but I didn't want to read page one again. It was boring enough the first time.

I clomped down the stairs with no idea what to expect.

"Hello, Brianna," Ms. Matheson said as soon as I got to the front hall. Apparently, Mom had asked her to come in.

"Hi, Ms. Matheson," I said politely. The way I talk to Mr. Lee. The way you are supposed to talk to school principals and presidents of neighborhood councils. Not the way I *wanted* to speak at that particular moment.

"Can we sit down and talk for a minute?" she said.

"Sure," I said hesitantly. I looked at Mom.

Mom smiled and turned back toward the kitchen. "Make yourselves comfortable in the living room," she said over her shoulder. "I'll make some tea." And then I was alone with the enemy.

Even though it was my house, Ms. Matheson led the way and I followed. She sat on the couch, and I perched on the end. I waited for her to speak. I was really curious about what she had to say. It must be big, for her to come here and speak to me as if I was a real person.

"I wanted you to know that you made an excellent presentation," Ms. Matheson said.

She looked at me, as if waiting for a reaction. I just looked back, trying hard not to give away any of the many emotions I was suddenly feeling.

"And I wanted to give you the results of the vote in person."

"Okay," I said quietly. It would be an understatement to say I was surprised. I didn't expect the results for a couple more days. And I certainly didn't expect to get them directly from Ms. Matheson.

"Here." She handed me a piece of paper. It was pee-colored.

My hands shook as I opened it.

Dear Residents of Cedar Grove,

This notice is to inform you that interim bylaw 47.21, which prohibited tree climbing within Cedar Grove Property, has failed ratification.

An updated list of current Cedar Grove bylaws is available on our website.

The Neighborhood Council would like to remind residents that parents are responsible for ensuring the safety of their children while on Cedar Grove property.

We would also like to recognize Brianna Bridges, Unit 83, for bringing the issue of tree-climbing safety forward for discussion. As noted in her presentation at the AGM, which is posted on our website, the risk of injury while climbing can be significantly reduced through education, supervision and adherence to a few basic rules. We are pleased that Brianna has

volunteered to continue offering basic tree-
climbing lessons to any interested residents.
Thank you all for your cooperation.
Sincerely,
Cedar Grove Neighborhood Council

I had to read the notice three times to make sure I got it right.

"So?" I still wasn't sure whether to laugh or cry.

"So, congratulations, Brianna," Ms. Matheson said.

"We can climb?"

Ms. Matheson didn't answer. Instead she asked, "Are you willing to continue offering basic tree-climbing lessons?"

Before I could reply, Mom came in with a tray of stuff for tea.

"How's it going?" Mom asked.

They were both looking at me, so I said, "Good... I think. Does this mean it's legal to climb all the trees?"

"Yes," Ms. Matheson said, "and we are really hoping you will help reduce the risk of injury by providing education and supervision like it says in the notice."

"Of course!" I said, the excitement practically bubbling out of me.

"Okay then," Ms. Matheson said as Mom poured the tea. No one spoke.

I wasn't sure what to do. I wanted to jump up and celebrate, but Mom had taught me it was rude to gloat. And I really did appreciate Ms. Matheson coming to give me the news in person, even if it was to ensure that I would continue providing lessons. I couldn't believe I was now being asked to do exactly what I didn't want to be caught doing just two short weeks ago.

The silence was bad. I felt like I was waiting in the principal's office.

My desperation to get out of the house finally won. Breaking the uncomfortable silence, I said, "Excuse me, but can I go?"

Ms. Matheson smiled, and Mom said, "Go where?"

"Climbing!" I jumped up, unable to contain my excitement anymore.

Mom looked over at Ms. Matheson who nodded and handed her the letter.

"Go," Mom said.

"Ethan's waiting for you," said Ms. Matheson.

I ran out the door and left them with their tea.

I could see Ethan in the tree as soon as I reached it.

"Come on up!" he yelled.

"I forgot how rough this one is," I said when I was finally perched on the branch next to him. I surveyed the scrapes left on my elbow by the tree's rough bark.

"I've named it Old Scratchy," Ethan said proudly.

"Good name."

"I bet you can't wait to tackle Mount Everest again," Ethan said, gesturing toward the tall tree beside us.

I nodded. "So your Mom explained it all to you?" I asked.

"She didn't have to," he said, "but she came out and watched me climb before going over to see you. She was really impressed. Said that tree climbing had given me confidence or something."

I looked at him and smiled.

"She also said…" Ethan hesitated.

"What?"

"That you should run for Neighborhood Council next year."

I rolled my eyes. "I think I'll join Tree Climbers International instead."

We both got a good laugh out of that. Then we started climbing higher.

And it was all legal.

Acknowledgments

Many thanks to Claire, for giving me the idea, helping brainstorm the plot and suffering through the very first draft: This story wouldn't exist without you. Thank you also to Jennifer Heath, for providing feedback, and to Sarah Harvey, for seeing the book's potential and holding my hand through the editing process. And finally, thank you to Oliver and Spencer, for inspiring my creativity, and to Tim, for your encouragement and support.

The mother of five-year-old twin boys, Yolanda Ridge writes whenever and wherever she gets a chance. She lives in Burnaby, British Columbia, near an old-growth forest, where the trees are much too big for her to climb. *Trouble in the Trees* is her first book. Visit her on the web at www.yolandaridge.com.